George Braithwaite

Life of Sôgorô, the farmer patriot of Sakura

George Braithwaite

Life of Sôgorô, the farmer patriot of Sakura

ISBN/EAN: 9783337303563

Printed in Europe, USA, Canada, Australia, Japan

Cover: Foto ©Raphael Reischuk / pixelio.de

More available books at **www.hansebooks.com**

LIFE OF SOGORO,

THE FARMER PATRIOT OF SAKURA,

TRANSLATED FROM THE JAPANESE

BY

GEORGE BRAITHWAITE.

———

WITH NINE ILLUSTRATIONS.

PRINTED

BY

THE YOKOHAMA BUNSHA.

—

1897.

TRANSLATOR'S PREFACE.

The particulars here given of the Life of Sogoro were first published in Japanese in 1887, being taken from an old manuscript written anonymously many years earlier. The book has had a large circulation.

In the course of study, the work was brought to my notice soon after it was issued. I went through it at once making a rough translation but little thinking it would ever be printed. In fact, the idea originated with those of my Japanese friends who went through the book with me. At first I was not inclined to adopt their suggestions, feeling as I do, that though the main facts of the story may be correct, the details cannot be so. The more I thought the matter over however, the more it seemed to me that the fact that it was a purely Japanese composition, giving a wonderful insight into Japanese ways of thought and action, would to some extent at least make up for its shortcomings in other respects. On this account, I have striven to adhere as closely to the original as the exigencies of the English language would allow, and have retained many expressions, which under other circumstances I should have dropped.

How enjoyable have been the hours spent in this work; and what added joy it will be should this story give pleasure to others, and be even to a small extent the means of arousing or increasing their interest in this land and its people! May the day soon come when the dwellers in this beautiful land shall know the love of the Lord Jesus Christ, receive Him as their Saviour, and rejoice in the sunshine of His love!

22, Takashima Yama,
    Kanagawa, Japan.   G. B.

June 1897.

PREFACE TO THE ORIGINAL JAPANESE EDITION.

To find truth in a farmer is, it is said, like running across a cherry-tree in a bamboo grove; and may
we not also say that to meet with treachery in a
warrior is like coming upon a bamboo growing among
cherry-trees? In a tumultuous age the government
showed no mercy, so much the more was there found
righteousness in the Province of Shimosa. How
illustrious and beautiful is that glorious name of
Sogoro; and how his fame still clings to the town of
Sakura! Indeed, the very name of this town, by having the same sound as the word for cherry, reminds
us of the beautiful cherry-flower, especially of the following kinds:—

THE MOONLIGHT MORNING CHERRY-FLOWER (Ariake-
sakura).
For, uninjured by the midnight storm, it always
looks most beautiful when in the early dawn the
dew on its leaves sparkles in the moonlight.
THE THREAD-LIKE CHERRY-FLOWER (Ito-sakura).
For it is cleansed by the dew as Sogoro was by
the thread of his deep petitions.
THE WATERFALL CHERRY-FLOWER (Taki-sakura).
For his wife's tears fell in torrents when he parted
from her, and thus caused the family-line to be
broken.

VI

The Infant Cherry-flower (Chigo-sakura).
For his heart went out to his infant children.
The Cloud-like Cherry-flower (Kumoi-sakura).
For his petition did not reach to the clouds (the
Emperor); and so he died, and became like
cherry-flowers scattered in clouds by the morn-
ing wind.
The Black Coloured Cherry-flower (Sumizome-
sakura).
For his fame still remains fragrant in writings.
The Cherry-tree (Sakura-ki).
For the blocks from which this book was printed
were made from a cherry-tree, and therefore the
whole tree remains; and the fact that a book-
seller has published it, and thus shown that he
is not behind the times, will bring glory to the
city where the whole flower of the nation
gathers.
After having seen the cherry-flowers at Yoshino and
Kiso, I returned to Tokyo; and took up my pen at
daybreak.

OTEI KINSHO.

CONTENTS.

VIII

LIST OF ILLUSTRATIONS.

LIFE OF SOGORO,

THE FARMER PATRIOT OF SAKURA.

CHAPTER I.

THE HOTTA FAMILY.

We read in Chinese History that, when king Buo died, Shuko took the reins of government, and at once sent for Shohakkin and said, "I am king Buo's brother and Buno's son, and thus am a man of no mean position ; and yet, so afraid am I of missing meeting the wise that one day, hearing callers while I was in my bath, I twisted up my hair and went out three times to see who had come. On another occasion, when at dinner, I went out several times to speak to visitors." After thus admonishing him, he sent him to Ro. It is still true now, as it was then, that all those who rule must be willing to put themselves to inconvenience to find out what is going on round them. Servants are often bent on amassing fortunes for themselves, and if their masters trust to them entirely, they will soon be ruined.

About two hundred and fifty years ago, there lived in Shimosa a noble named Hotta Kozuke no Suke—the lord of the castle of Sakura. His grandfather Hotta Kwanemon was one of Hideaki's trusty officers and a member of the Cabinet. The Shogun Hidetada treated him with great kindness, and made his son Shogoro one of his constant attendants; and such a favourite was he, that he gave him the castle of Sakura with an annual income of 120,000 koku of rice, and called him Hotta Kaga no Kami Masamori. On his becoming a member of the Cabinet, he proved himself so faithful that the country was to be congratulated on having secured the services of such a useful man.

On the death of the Shogun, the whole nation lost heart and seemed for a time like men out without lanterns on a dark night. His attendants felt it more than others, for they had waited upon him for years and basked in the sunshine of his favour; and now stupefied with grief, they wandered about like rudderless ships in the middle of the ocean. Thirty-six of them, led by Hotta Masamori, committed suicide together and thus went to attend their master in the next world. The stone monument commemorating their devotion may still be seen on one of the hills near Nikko. Such fidelity as theirs is rare even in Japan and China, and so an increase of salary was given to each of their descendants. Kozuke no Suke had been high in favour before; but now, as Hotta Masamori's heir, he was treated with special kindness and was given the positions that his father had filled.

Several hundred years before this time, about A. D. 935, Hanai Gondayu one of Sogoro's ancestors had by his bravery and courage made his name justly famous. He

belonged to the emperor's body-guard and was appointed
to attend his daughter. Shortly after his appointment,
she was seized with leprosy and was sent to Shimosa ;
it being feared that, if she stayed at the palace, the
three sacred treasures would become infected. Hanai
Gondayu went with her, had a palace built for her in the
district of Innan and devoted himself to nursing her.
Just before her death, she called him to her and said :
" I feel grateful to the emperor that I was born a
princess ; but am not conscious of having, in a previous
state of existence, done anything deserving of punishment ; and so cannot understand why I should have had
this terrible disease, and been forced by it to live in this
out of the way place. I have felt some of the sufferings
that all women are subject to and from which many die ;
and so after my death, I swear that all who pray to me
shall certainly be relieved." With these words she
passed away. Hanai Gondayu felt her death very
much and buried her with respect amid many tears.
She was deified some years later and certain it is that
prayers made to her are nearly always answered, for
many women can testify to having received most
wonderful cures.

After her death Hanai Gondayu did not feel inclined
to enter into service again, but made up his mind to
live at ease and went and settled at Iwahashi changing
his name to Sodayu. He mingled with the villagers
and in a few years married, and thus became the
ancestor of Sozaemon, an incident from whose life
is related in the following chapter.

CHAPTER II.

SOZAEMON QUARRELS WITH A POTATOE SELLER.

Sozaemon, the grandfather of our hero, was a kind, large-hearted man ; but had unfortunately a very quick temper. This often led him into quarrels, and might have caused much trouble, had not the authorities been very strict with him and always settled each case promptly. One day, about the middle of Keicho [1605], a farmer stopped at his door and asked him to buy some potatoes. Sozaemon wanted a great many, but all except seven or eight had been already sold. These he bought and paid for, but found when he took them that some of them had been broken in two and mended with bamboo skewers and the join concealed with earth. Seeing that, he got angry and accused the farmer of trying to deceive him. The farmer replied : "They are just as good ! You are going to make them into broth so they will have to be cut up small any way." "It is my own concern," Sozaemon said, " whether I make them into broth or not. When you found them broken, you should have left them so, you rascal, instead of mending them as you have done to deceive people." At that, the farmer became very angry too and said : " I am surprised you should call me a rascal. We both have eyes. I was not trading with a blind man." This made Sozaemon still more angry and, clenching his fist, he hit the farmer violently on the head. Much to his astonishment the farmer fell back at once and became insensible. Completely sobered by this, Sozaemon did his best to restore him but for some time his efforts seemed in vain, he showed no signs of returning consciousness. At last however, his toes began trembling a little, and all of a sudden he jumped up and stared vacantly about. Sozaemon was very glad, and after telling him what had happened said : " How troubled we all should have been if you had died from that blow ! How do you feel now ?" The farmer scratched his head and said : " I am very subject to these attacks, but I soon recover and am as well as usual directly. I am very sorry to have alarmed your family and must ask you kindly to excuse it." Sozaemon feeling quite relieved said : " I am so glad to hear you say so. You must take something before you go." He gave him some wine and food ; also the money for the potatoes and a little extra, and a piece of cotton besides. The farmer declined the presents three or four times, but at last took them ; and, putting his baskets across his shoulder, took his leave and started home in thoroughly good humour.

His road lay across the Hirakawa Ferry—kept by a man named Tahei, who made a scanty living by ferrying people across. It was just the end of autumn, and there were so few travellers that he could not earn enough to buy food ; and was in great straits. Much pleased to see the potatoe-seller come up, he prepared to row him across. As they were crossing, the potatoe-seller told him about his quarrel at Iwahashi. To this Tahei listened eagerly, trying to find some way of get-

ting some money. At last he said to the potatoe-seller:
" That is a beautiful piece of cotton you have. Please
sell it to me as I wish to make it into clothes for the
winter. I will leave the price to you but as the proverb
says, Nothing can be settled without a consulation."
The farmer thought a while and then said : " It would
be very easy to sell it but I do not like to as it was given
me by the headman of Iwahashi." Tahei laughed and
said : " You farmers have only one idea and do not know
every thing. Cotton can only be used for clothes, but
if you sell it, you can buy rice or anything else you
like with the money, and in that way you might get a
present that you liked better." After a little thought,
the farmer said he would sell it ; and Tahei quite set
up gave him the money at once. As the farmer stepped
out of the boat, he muttered to himself : " Oh ! what a
nuisance these baskets are !" Tahei overheard him and
said he ought not to say so ; but he burst out laughing
and said : " I shall get rid of them as soon as I reach
home. You won't catch me coming this way again."
Delighted to hear that, Tahei offered to buy them. The
farmer agreed at once and selling them for a trifle
hurried away home.

In the meantime Sozaemon was congratulating himself on having settled that day's difficulty so easily.
Just before he went to bed however, some one knocked loudly at his door. Inquiring who it was, he was
told that Tahei, the Hirakawa ferryman had come and
wished to see him on important business. Filled
with surprise and not a little curious to hear what
had happened, he told his servant to invite him in.

TAHEI BLACKMAILING SOZAEMON.

Page 7.

On his asking what was the matter, Tahei took out the piece of cotton and asked him whether he had ever seen it before. Recognizing it at once as the very piece he had given to the farmer, Sozaemon told him all that had taken place. Tahei hearing that, said : "About sunset, a potatoe-seller carrying two baskets across his shoulder took the ferry-boat; but when about half way across he suddenly became insensible. I was much surprised and took him home and nursed him as well as I could. At last he came to himself and said : 'Mr. Sozaemon of Iwahashi struck me violently today, and stunned me, but I soon recovered. At first I had no pain ; but after I started, my head began to hurt me and got worse and worse, until when I reached here I could go no further and now I shall die here. I am a green-grocer and live in Hongo in Yedo. My name is Kyubei, and I must trouble you to let my wife and children know about my death.' While speaking, he was seized with a fit of coughing and died almost directly. I found this piece of cotton in one of his baskets, and brought it here at once, as I thought that if his story was true, it would bring you into trouble." Sozaemon's face was ashen white as he listened, and his whole body was bathed in perspiration ; but, seeing no way out of the difficulty, he thanked Tahei for so kindly informing him ; and then asked whether he had any plan to suggest. This was just what Tahei wanted, but not wishing to show it, he appeared lost in thought for several minutes and then said : "It is very difficult to think of any plan, but I am the only one so far who knows anything about it, so if I say nothing no one else will find out. I will go back and bury the body at once. Fortunately it is late, and no one is likely to see me at work." Sozaemon was much pleased and said : " If it should get known, it would disgrace not only my whole family, but the village too. I cannot repay your kindness but must give you what I can." So saying, he took out twenty ryo. Tahei averred it was too much, but put it in his bosom ; and taking his leave, hastened back to the ferry. For a short time he was very happy and gave himself up to pleasure ; but it was money obtained by roguery, and so was soon spent ; and he was again plunged into poverty, and could buy neither food nor clothing. Sozaemon felt very sorry for him and helped him repeatedly. At bottom, Tahei was not really bad, and this kindness touched his heart and made him repent of his terrible sin and turn over a new leaf.

Now Sozaemon had an apprentice, named Sakichi who was just fifteen. Sozaemon had shaved off his forelock for him, and had shown him repeated kindnesses, letting him wait on him morning and evening. Though too young to do much mischief, he was very cunning and perverse ; and, being in the next room at the time, had overheard his master's conversation with Tahei, and was treasuring it up in his heart till he found a good opportunity of frightening his master by telling him about it. One day seeing ten ryo in his master's room, he took it. When Sozaemon found it out and began scolding him, he did not seem at all confused ; but told what he knew about the potatoe-seller, and threatened if scolded any more to make the story public. Much surprised, Sozaemon begged him not to tell any one else about it, and told him he could keep the ten ryo he had taken. Sakichi thanked him, but thought that Sozaemon really could not help himself; and so after that, he held his head higher than ever. Sozaemon often felt vexed with him; but overlooked his rudeness, not wishing to drive him to extremities.

One day meeting Tahei, he told him how Sakichi knew his secret, and how insolently he was behaving. After reaching his home, Tahei thought the matter over carefully and said to himself: "It is all my fault that he is so anxious, and that such wicked ideas have got into his servant's heart. Had I not better confess everything and set his mind at rest? What I told him about the potatoe-seller belonging to Hongo in Yedo was quite false. I have no idea where to look for him, but I will keep my eyes open and see whether he comes this way again. I must prove that he is still living, before I can ask Sozaemon to forgive me."

Sakichi, seeing he could frighten Sozaemon so easily, planned to swindle him well, and then run off and live in comfort. One day therefore he said to him : "I am ill and find my work too hard. Please give me a hundred ryo and let me go home and nurse for a few weeks. If you won't do this I will summon you." Sozaemon had borne with him so long that he lost his temper as soon as he heard that and cried out: "Have you forgotten how you came here when you were quite a child, and how kindly I have always treated you? It is extremely rude of you to ask to leave at all, but far more so to ask so impolitely. You are however only an apprentice, and not worth grieving over ; so I will dismiss you as you request, but you shall not have any money. Be quick and clear out ! You are not fit to be called a man !" When he had finished speaking, he got up without waiting for a reply, and went into the next room. " I will make you repent before you are many days older ! " shouted Sakichi as he rushed from the house in a fury.

Going straight to the court house, he there entered a complaint against his master. Sozaemon was much surprised, but felt it useless to worry himself unduly, as it had all been caused by his own quick temper. Just as he was starting to go to the Office, Tahei ran panting up and said : " How anxious you must be about this summons. Let me go with you. I will clear it up if it costs me my life. The potatoe-seller is still living. I was very hard up at the time and deceived you." Sozaemon was much surprised to hear that and said : " I had no idea of that, had I known it before, all this trouble might have been prevented. However come with me now to the court and tell all you know there."

On their arrival the governor pointed to Sakichi and said to Sozaemon : " Do you know that man ? He accuses you of striking and killing a farmer last year in a fit of passion while he was selling you some potatoes, and of having the body buried secretly ; but you no doubt remember all about it." Just then Tahei stepped forward and said : " I am the Hirakawa ferryman and I beg to state that that accusation is not true. It all arose from my being so poor at the time that I could not buy food; so I concocted the whole story and swindled Sozaemon out of twenty ryo. No one is to blame but me, so please punish me according to law." Here Sakichi interposed and said : " I have to state that this ferryman has been helped by my master repeatedly, and in return wishes to bear his punishment, the scoundrel. What he has just told you is false; otherwise the potatoe-seller must still be living." Tahei looked at Sakichi fiercely and said : " You went to Sozaemon when you were only a child and he has treated you most kindly. It is monstrous of you to summon such a master! What will you do if the potatoe-seller is still living?" Sakichi answered : " I have as you say been most kindly treated by my master; but what difference does that make? When he commits a crime he becomes a criminal. I felt it my duty therefore to bring him before the court, knowing that if such crimes were allowed to go unpunished, they would only increase. If the potatoe-seller is still living, bring him here and prove your innocence." Here the governor broke in and said : " You must all of you leave the court now, and stay in your homes handcuffed until I send for you. Heaven can make all plain." As Sozaemon was such a good man, his friends felt sure that Heaven would protect him.

One day not long after, the potatoe-seller stopped at Sozaemon's house and said : " I am so much obliged to you for all your kindness to me last winter. I should have come to thank you before, but have been ill since and so could not do so. I hope however you will accept these as a little return for all you have done." So saying, he took out some potatoes. Sozaemon took them and said : "After you went away, I was accused of killing you ; and now there are three people handcuffed, and confined to their homes on your account." The farmer was much astonished to hear that and said : "It is all my fault, as it all arose out of my selling the piece of cotton you gave me. I will go to the court and confess. I am a greengrocer named Shosaku and live in Senju." On seeing him, the governor at once summoned the three men and said : "Now the potatoe-seller has been produced, there is no room left for doubting Tahei's words. All this trouble arose in the first place from the story he made up, but he has turned over a new leaf, and so is let off with a small fine. As for the twenty ryo he got from Sozaemon, they must settle that themselves. Sakichi deserves to be put to death for having so basely accused his master on such slight grounds ; but, by the exercise of extraordinary clemency, he is only sentenced to be banished. Sozae-mon is unpunished ; but as his quick temper caused all this trouble, he is severely reprimanded. The potatoe-seller is innocent." As they went home, Sozaemon told Tahei he might keep the twenty ryo, and thus made Tahei admire him more than ever.

Sozaemon saw that his quick temper would give him a great deal of trouble if he could not overcome it ; so he wrote the word "Patience" on a tablet, and hung it in his room ; and as he looked at it day after day, he gradually managed to conquer his temper and to live in peace with his family and neighbours ; and thus the word

" Patience " was handed down to his descendants.   His
son Sobei succeeded him, and he in turn was succeeded
by his son Sogoro, who is thus known to be Sozaemon's
grandson.   This story is given here as it was one of
the principal incidents in the history of Sogoro's ancestors.   Some of his biographers say he was descended
from Heishino Masakado ; and others that he came
originally from Higo, and was adopted by Sozaemon.
Both these statements are equally incredible.   In my
opinion, there seems no doubt that his ancestors for
many generations back were farmers.

Supposed representation of the Tablet which Sozaemon,
Sogoro's grandfather wrote.
The Chinese character signifies " Patience."

CHAPTER. III.

THE WONDERFUL MONSTER OF IMBA MARSH.

Now in the Province of Shimosa, is a large lake called Imba Marsh. It is twenty miles long and more than twelve miles wide, and is therefore the largest in the Eastern Provinces. The view from it on a clear day is very fine. The great river Tone flows through it ; and on the left may be seen the top of Mount Tsukuba; and on the right the tiled roofs of the villages of Nakagawa, Shusui, and Sakura. The lovely peak of Fuji is visible to the southwest with numerous villages clustering at its foot and dotting the plain; while on the sea between, numbers of fishing boats rise and fall gracefully on the waves. On the shore of the lake is the village of Yoshitaka, clustering round the spacious temple of Kofukuji with its handsome pagoda. The roof of the temple stands out conspicuous among the thick trees that adorn the shore. At the time of our story, it was in the charge of a priest of the Zenshu sect. He followed the teachings of Ikkyu Takuan, and never tired of looking at the flowers and the stars, and thus studying nature ; and being celebrated for his stores of virtue and wisdom accumulated by no less than thirty-six generations of virtuous ancestors, had a large number of disciples.

Our hero Sogoro was at this time called Kenmatsu, and was sent to the temple to be educated. Though only eight years old, he was so clever and quick that if he heard one Chinese character he seemed to know ten, and so was soon able to read and write. In two or three years, he had learnt many books by heart; and could also sing and compose poetry. The priest was very fond of him and said he was an extraordinary child.

Among the lads, who came to the temple to study, was one named Tsunetaro. He was only thirteen and so was a year younger than Kenmatsu; but being very clever, he made up his mind to beat him. This put Kenmatsu on his mettle; and so they both did their utmost, and gave their whole minds to their studies; and thus their progress was extremely rapid. Tsunetaro was very strong and brave, afraid of nothing; but as for Kenmatsu, he was so timid that he very rarely ventured out alone even in the day time; and he was always terribly frightened when it got dark; moreover so quiet and gentle was he that most who knew him said he was a fool. The villagers used often to discuss the merits of the two, and were pretty well agreed that Tsunetaro was the braver and more talented lad; the priests at the temple however preferred Kenmatsu, and maintained that he had the finer character.

Now, in the middle of Imba Marsh, is a place of great depth known as Sakuchi Ana; and just above this spot, flashes of light might be seen at night. As these continued month after month, and year after year, all the people round talked of nothing else; and became at last so terrified that they would not stir out after dark. Some talked of asking their lord to come and destroy the monster; others of getting some celebrated priest to drive it away. When one dog barks, all the others, it is said, join in ; and in the same way the excitement spread from village to village, until the whole district was in a fever. One day, seven or eight of the villagers chanced to meet at the Kofukuji temple ; and one of them said, a dragon had been seen above the hole, about a hundred feet long with terrible shining scales ; another said that one of his friends had seen numbers of women, breathing flames and running about on the water with their hair all flying in the wind ; and he added that wherever they went, they brought famine and pestilence. The villagers were much alarmed and spent a long time discussing how to ward off the fearful dangers that seemed to threaten them.

Kenmatsu and Tsunetaro were sitting by the fire listening. As usual, Kenmatsu was silent, but Tsunetaro pressed forward, and asked those who had spoken whether they had themselves seen what they had just narrated. They replied that they had not done so, but had seen those who had, and so there could be no mistake about it. Tsunetaro laughed and said : "I cannot credit your stories. Such tales are hardly ever true. But how is it that you have none of you gone and examined the place ?" Hearing that they said : "You must be joking. It is in the middle of a large lake, of which indeed it is the source, and is so deep that the water all the time rushes out with great force. In ordinary times it is not safe to go there, but it is far more dangerous now, while such a monster is living there, coming out every evening and frightening everybody." Tsunetaro replied : "If

you say so it will always trouble you, so to-morrow
night I shall go myself and stop its pranks." When
they heard that, they all burst out laughing and said :
" How boldly you talk! You are but a lad ! How
can you accomplish what we dare not even attempt ?"
Tsunetaro laughed and said : " One's courage is not
always in proportion to his age. We will not discuss it
further. To-morrow night you shall see the terrible
monster for yourselves." The others did not reply and
so they all separated for the night.

The next evening, as he watched the sun nearing
the western hills, Tsunetaro braced up his courage
with the hope of destroying the monster, and thus
saving all the people in the neighbourhood from
their fears. Hardly had the sun set and the sky
become clouded over with the evening darkness, when a
small boat pushed aside the reeds on the margin of the
lake. The man in it had a gun, a bow, and a sword.
Pushing out some distance from the shore, he saw, as
all had said, a light flashing at times from the neighbourhood of Sakuchi Ana and rising to the sky. An ordinary man would have been terrified and have fainted
directly ; but Tsunetaro being courageous and bold, was
not the least disturbed. Looking round, he saw some
one in a small boat a little way in front watching the
light, and said to himself : " That is strange. The
spectre has transformed itself into a man. I will shoot
it." Going nearer he heard a cough, and a low voice said:
" Is not that Tsunetaro ?" Much surprised he looked
carefully, and seeing Kenmatsu, said : " Mr. Kenmatsu,
why did you come alone and steal a march on me ?"

He replied : " Last night I noticed you said that you were going in order to save the people further trouble, and this made me wish to go too. I felt sure however you would refuse to have me for a companion if I asked you ; and so I came by myself, and have just finished examining the place." Remembering how much Kenmatsu disliked going out alone, and how terribly afraid he always was of the darkness ; Tsunetaro was astounded, and admired the motives which had enabled him to overcome his feelings so effectually. They soon lashed their boats together and while they did so, the light rose from the hole and shone across the surface of the water, making their bodies and hair glisten. Tsunetaro seized his gun to shoot, but Kenmatsu said : " Wait a little. There are three kinds of light, male, female, and spiritual. I examined it before you came and saw that it is not any of these, but is only a reflection in the sky from something in the water. Rotten wood or fish scales give out light at night, and this looks to me as if it came from fish scales. The man who shoots without knowing at what he is shoot- ing is called a coward, and will be laughed at as such : so please let me try another way first." With these words, he made Tsunetaro take the pole, and looking carefully at the place where the light was, took up a net and threw it into the water, whereupon the light disappeared immediately. The two men then tried to pull up the net, but found it as heavy as a large rock ; by pulling both together however, they at last managed to get it into the boat, and saw they had caught a huge mullet. Much pleased, they rowed

CATCHING THE MONSTER.

back as fast as they could. The villagers not having seen them all the evening, concluded they had gone to the marsh, and felt quite ashamed to think how they had insulted and laughed at Tsunetaro the evening before. Great therefore was their confusion and shame when they saw him and Kenmatsu coming back in triumph. The mullet was more than three feet long; and all the people were amazed at its size, and at once saw that it had caused the light. They praised the young men for what they had done, but were particularly struck with the courage and reflection Kenmatsu had shown. As no more was heard of the horrible monster, the whole country-side felt greatly relieved; and all the people praised the two lads for their courage, and for having freed them from the terrible dread which had hung over them so long.

Tsunetaro went back to the temple, feeling very happy; and was soon fast asleep. When he woke the next morning, he thought to himself: "What a fool I have been all along to think Kenmatsu was a coward when really he was full of courage and was only a little shy. The skill he showed in always hiding his wisdom and courage is equal to that displayed by any of the old heroes. I do not believe he would be the least bit frightened even though he suddenly found himself surrounded by enemies. After laughing so much at him for being so easily scared, I feel quite ashamed to think how cowardly I was last night, not daring to go unarmed; while he, brave man that he is, looked calmly into the water, and acted all through as though there was nothing to be afraid of. He is certainly a true hero."

With these thoughts, he invited Kenmatsu into his room, and said : " However shameful you may consider my past conduct, please condescend to take the seat of honour as I have something to ask you." Quite taken by surprise, Kenmatsu said : " Mr. Tsunetaro, why are you so polite ? We have always been firm friends, and I cannot understand why you should change so suddenly." Tsunetaro burst into tears and replied : " I am thoroughly ashamed of myself for the shabby way in which I have treated you, and can hardly speak of it ; I could not perceive your great generosity with my common eyes, but I implore you to forgive my past shortcomings and allow me to become your younger brother. Let us follow the example of those who swore an oath of friendship in the peach garden, and I will ask you graciously to grant me an oath to die on the same day." He spoke very earnestly. When he had finished, Kenmatsu said : " Though I am astonished at your request, I am quite willing to swear an oath of friendship as you propose. I must however positively refuse to become your older brother, so please excuse me." Tsunetaro shook his head and said : " No, no, not so. All the rest of my life I shall look upon you as my older brother, and shall be sadly offended if you refuse. I am in earnest." With these words, he forced him to take the place of honour, and quickly brought out the wine and food he had prepared for the occasion. They each then took a short sword ; and cutting their arms, let the blood from the two wounds mingle in the same cup, and swore that though they had not been born on the same day,

they would henceforth be brothers, and would both die
on the same day.

As they swore, the sliding screen was suddenly
pushed back and some one entered the room. Looking up, what was their surprise and fright to see it
was the high priest! Greeting them with a smile, he
said: "Good luck to your oath of friendship! You,
Tsunetaro, are naturally proud of your courage, and
have often gone wrong and made me quite anxious;
but if you are careful to follow Kenmatsu's example,
you will do well. You, Kenmatsu, can do a great deal
of good if you do not yield too easily to your noble
desires to sacrifice your own comfort for that of others.
You are now both men, and I will change your names.
Kenmatsu is a dragon among men, so he ought to be
the leader and shall be called Sogoro; while you,
Tsunetaro shall be called Chuzo." Both men were very
glad and promised to attend to his advice; and said
they hoped to have an opportunity some time of repay-
ing his kindness, which they said was deeper than the
sea. After studying for another year at the temple, they
returned to their native places and there busied themselves assiduously with household occupations. They
cared for their parents, were faithful to their friends,
kind to the young, and reverential to the aged, so that
all who knew them respected them highly.

CHAPTER IV.

A Wrestling Match.

There is, near the town of Sakura, a hill called Mount Masakado, so named after Soma Kojiro, who about the middle of the 10th century raised the standard of rebellion, built himself a castle, and proclaimed himself king under the name of Masakado. He attacked and conquered the eight provinces east of Hakone, but at last his castle was taken and destroyed, and he himself was killed in battle. In honour of those who then perished, a Wrestling Match is held every autumn on Mount Masakado. To this the young people of the district always come in crowds, and most interesting it is to watch them wrestling with one another. After all the pairs have finished, there is a final struggle to see who is the real victor for the day. This is called the " Final Wrestle." If any one then manages to throw three others in succession, he is rewarded with a piece of silk, but it will be seen that unless he is very strong, he cannot hope to win.

At the time of our history, the games were held as usual; and at half-past two—the hour for the final bout—the victors for the day assembled to try their strength. One of them, whose name was Okuma, soon threw two of the others, and so felt quite confident of the victory as he only had one more to throw. Among the spectators was a man named Tenjinyama, a great favourite among the villagers. Arawashi, one of his apprentices, a celebrated wrestler and well up to all the dodges, seeing Okuma so successful and wishing to beat him, leapt into the ring, saying : " Come on, let us have a try ! " Okuma said : " All right." They seemed well matched, and as soon as the umpire gave the signal by drawing back his fan, they rushed at each other without losing a moment. Arawashi tried to seize his opponent ; but he, perceiving his purpose, caught him with his left hand, though the effort made him breathe hard. Noticing this, Arawashi suddenly twisted round, and threw him on his head right in the middle of the ring.

At that, the spectators cheered loudly ; and Tenjinyama and all his apprentices stood fanning themselves, and leaping for joy as they thought that surely no one else would attempt to wrestle with their comrade after the wonderful skill he had just shown. Very soon however, a young man of about eighteen or nineteen named Suijinyama challenged him. Arawashi accepted the challenge and seized him, hoping to conquer him at the first try, but though he did not look so, he was extremely strong and very skilful and active too. For a little while they struggled like lions without either gaining any apparent advantage. Then Arawashi, pretending to be tired out, made Suijinyama put forth all his strength, and dodging as he did so, forced him out of the ring. Arawashi now felt quite sure of the prize, not thinking any one else would dare to wrestle with him.

Now Takasu, a great friend of Suijinyama's, had

been watching the contests eagerly for some time. On
seeing his friend beaten he sprang into the ring, saying: "Let us try who will conquer!" Arawashi
thought from his look that he was no wrestler, and
spreading out his arms, said, chuckling: "I do not
mind how many of your sort I wrestle with. Come
on!" After they had wrestled a little while Arawashi, having seized his opponent's belt, they both
fell to the ground together. Seeing that, Takasu's
party jumped for joy and said: "Our man has beat-
en! Our man has beaten!" But Arawashi's friends
said: "No, no, we have beaten!" The umpire was
appealed to; but was unable to settle it, and so it was
decided that they should wrestle again. Takasu made
up his mind to try some of his dodges and not allow
his adversary to seize his belt as he had done before.
As soon as the signal was given, Arawashi rushed at
him, but he dodging to the right, put forth all his
strength, and threw him in grand style right out of the
ring. The spectators jumped up and cried out:
"Well done, that's clever." Takasu's friends were extremely glad and cried out boastingly: "Does Mr.
Arawashi wish to wrestle any more? We really conquered the first time, and he who is twice victor goes
away justly victor." Tenjinyama's company were
much vexed, but could do nothing as no one else would
challenge Takasu; and so at last, he took that day's
bow, and as it was getting late, they all dispersed.

As Takasu was quietly going home, some rough looking men suddenly rushed out at him from a bamboo
grove, and called out: "Stop! Stop! Mr. Arawashi

is vexed at the result of the wrestling to-day, and has made up his mind to settle it at the point of the sword." Takasu laughed and said : " A man wrestles on the impulse of the moment and not out of malice. It is unmanly in him to be so vexed at having been beaten, but if he wishes to fight I am ready to accommodate him. Come on! Come on!" Hardly had he spoken, when fifteen or sixteen men rushed on him with drawn swords, determined apparently not to let him escape. Having practised fencing all his life, he was not at all disheartened and parried their blows so skilfully and made so many cuts at them that before long they were all scared and did not care to go near him. Tenjinyama and Arawashi took no part at first ; but when they saw how Takasu was getting the best of it, they both rushed to attack him. His friends had all gone on in front, but ran back to help him as soon as they heard of the attack, so that in a few moments there would have been a great fight.

Now Sogoro had inherited his father's property and was headman of the village of Iwahashi. He had gone to keep order at the wrestling match and was on his way home when he heard of the fight. Losing no time, he galloped to the place and jumped in among the naked swords, shouting : " Stop! Stop! I am Sogoro of Iwahashi and can settle this. Let me try." One word from him was like the voice of the stork, and all the combatants immediately sheathed their swords. Delighted at that, he said : " Mr. Tenjinyama has no just cause for resentment against Mr. Takasu for conquering his friend Mr. Arawashi. Mr. Arawashi had

beaten both Messrs. Okuma and Suijinyama before, and
they have just as much reason for being angry with
him. If wrestling gave rise to quarrels in this way, it
would have to be done away with altogether. Such
childish behaviour as that exhibited by the illustrious
Messrs. Tenjinyama and Arawashi, I never dreamt
of seeing. Much ashamed and crest-fallen, they said :
" We have, as you say, acted extremely foolishly.
Your advice is extremely good, and we thank you
a thousand times for your trouble." Takasu bowed,
and then both parties swore to let the matter drop,
and drank and chatted freely together.

That night Takasu thought over the kind way in
which Sogoro had come to his rescue, and determined
to become his retainer and work with him. The next
day therefore, he went to Iwahashi to see him. Sogoro
was fortunately at home and asked him into his back
room. Takasu said : " I can find no words with
which to thank you for your great kindness yesterday.
But for your timely help, I should never have got home
alive, so I hope you will kindly accept this small present I have brought." Sogoro replied : " You should
not have troubled to bring me such a beautiful present ;
you make far too much of such a trifling matter. I am
very glad to be able to congratulate you on your safety.
You are worth any number of such profligate, wicked,
good for nothing fellows as those who attacked you
yesterday. Hereafter you must be more cautious."
" Thank you much," said Takasu, " in future I intend
to take more care of myself. This present is very
small, but I shall not be satisfied unless you take it.

I have a matter to lay before you in which I am
very anxious to get your assistance. As you are
doubtless aware, I was separated from my parents
when I was only a child, and can get no help from
any of my other relations. For some time past, I
have felt that I ought to have some friend I could
rely on. Often have I heard of your great wisdom,
and much do I admire the depth of your since-
rity and ability; so please allow me to swear an
oath of friendship, and look upon you from this time
as my parent and older brother." As he finished
speaking, he knelt down and looked so enthusiastic
that Sogoro admired him and said : " I feel myself
altogether undeserving of your confidence ; but if you
wish, we will become brothers for the future. I am
however very sorry that you should ask me to become
your parent and older brother as I am quite unworthy."
Takasu said " No, no, not so ; your goodness is already
well known and you are well on in years ; so let it be
as I say, and I will reverence you as my older brother.
Please yield to my desire and graciously give your
consent." Just then a young man came out from
behind the screen and said : " Mr. Takasu's request
is right from top to bottom. Please consent to it,
brother, and then we three shall be able to talk over
everything together." Takasu was much pleased to
make the acquaintance of this man, who, as the reader
has doubtless guessed, was no other than Chuzo of
Chiba. Before separating, these three heroes made
a feast together—Sogoro was older brother, Chuzo
was next, and Takasu was the youngest, changing his

name of Toragoro to Saburobe. After talking and laughing the whole day and night, they parted.

CHAPTER V.

TAKASU FIGHTS A DUEL WITH JUSABURO.

In the province of Shimosa there is a village, called Kazuta, and near it in old days was a pool known in poetry as the Pool of Kazumada. Though at one time quite celebrated, it has long since dried up, and now only the name remains. At the time of which we write, there lived in the village, a wealthy farmer named Todayu, who had two daughters. One of them was married and attended to the house; the other, whose name was Oran, was only sixteen and was kept in seclusion in a back room. She had a beautiful form and a slender waist, and was altogether so graceful in her movements that she was considered by far the most attractive girl in the neighbourhood. She was also a good musician and knew many poems by heart. In autumn, she would go out to see the maple trees, and dearly loved to meditate in the moonlight; and in spring, how she did grieve when the rough winds scattered the flowers which the nightingales so delight in ! She was a general favourite, and it is not surprising therefore that Takasu fell in love with her the first time they met. From that day he could think of no one else even in his dreams, and sent her numberless letters but never received any answers. It is said that even brocade becomes rotten ; and the fine linen that gives so much pleasure one day, only brings trouble the next ; and so Takasu lived all alone in his cheerless room, lamenting and grieving that he had only the dull moon to keep him company. One night it seemed more than he could bear, so he got up and sent Oran the following song :—

> If I this night for you should die,
> Where alas could my body lie?
> Of the Pool of Kazumada,
> Not e'en the smallest drops remain,
> Where I can float and end my pain.

Truly Tsurayuki spoke the truth when he said that the gods look down in compassion on men and women and reconcile them to each other; and so it came to pass in this instance. Oran was much affected by the song Takasu had sent her, and it softened her heart so much that she longed to see him and sent him the following reply :—

> Sometimes deep and sometimes shallow,
> In this world of change and sorrow,
> Is the Pool of Kazumada :
> Who will not therein wet his sleeve,
> In truth comes only to deceive.

On receiving this song, Takasu felt as though he had suddenly been transported to the seventh heaven and went that night to Oran's room. They swore eternal love to one another and met again and again ; till at

last reports of their intimacy got out : for it is said
that a bad thing is known a thousand miles off ; and so
without any one saying a word, it spread abroad.

Now there was living in the immediate neighbourhood a young man named Jusaburo.   He was a
distant relation of Oran's, and ever since their childhood
their parents had jokingly said that they were to marry
each other.   Oran had become so beautiful as she
grew up that Jusaburo was quite willing to marry her,
and so the villagers spoke of them almost as though
they were already married.   Hearing the reports about
how she was going on, Jusaburo sent one of his friends
to make further enquiries.   Finding the stories true,
he was extremely angry and resolved to pay Takasu
out.   "I should like," thought he, "to kill him at once,
but he is a warrior and will have to be treated as such.
If I am cowardly and kill him by stealth or ask any
of my friends to help me I shall bring dishonour on
my name and descendants.   I will therefore send him
a challenge."   He accordingly sat down and wrote as
follows :—

> Mr. Takasu, having heard about your meet-
> ings with Miss Oran, I have made enquiries
> and found the reports quite true.   She and
> I have been as good as engaged to each
> other all our lives, and if this report of your
> conduct becomes generally known, it will
> bring me into disgrace.   I therefore hereby
> challenge you to a duel with swords.
>
> KAZUTA JUSABURO.
> 2nd Year of Kwanei [Aug. 1625].

Takasu was much surprised to receive such a challenge, but knowing it was useless to attempt any explanation, he agreed to fight and at once sent the original to Sogoro together with his answer and the following note:—

> This duel cannot be avoided and so it is no good for me to try and get off by apologizing to Jusaburo. He seems a straightforward man and has as you see sent me a regular challenge. I have therefore committed myself to the care of Heaven. At first I thought of not mentioning it to anybody even to you, as he will not of course allow me to have anyone to help me; but I was afraid you might be angry if I did not and you only found it out afterwards.

After sending the above, Takasu hastened to Kazuta Common. It was the middle of August and a clear night; so as he ran, he had the moon, the sky, and his heart, for companions. On reaching the Common, he could hear the monotonous humming of the insects, and noticed the luxuriant growth of the tall grasses; but, not seeing any sign of his opponent, he began to wonder whether after all he had not turned coward. While waiting, he wiped away the sweat, and then took out his pipe and began smoking. Hardly had he done so, when he noticed a thick cluster of grass and reeds near him suddenly divide; and a young man came in sight, shouting: "I suppose you are Mr. Takasu. I had a good way to come but have been waiting here a long

while for you." " I started," answered Takasu, " directly your letter came, and am very sorry to have kept
you waiting." Jusaburo thought he would have a
smoke before fighting, and so took out his pipe and
said : " Please let me have some tobacco and matches."
Takasu said : " You and I are going to fight directly
and do our best to kill one another, why then do you
ask me for anything ? " Jusaburo burst out laughing
and said : " So, so, what a narrow-minded man you
must be to talk like that ! A duel is a duel ; and
tobacco is tobacco." Quite taken aback at this,
Takasu handed him the tobacco at once. Jusaburo
thanked him and smoked for a few minutes in silence.
When he had finished, they both rose ; and unsheathing
their swords, began the fight. They fought with great
ferocity, but though they both tried their utmost,
neither gained any advantage ; in fact, they seemed to
fight like fire and water.

Now Sogoro was at home when Takasu's letter
reached him ; and was greatly surprised to hear how
matters stood, never having suspected anything of the
kind. Sure that unless the duel was stopped, one of
them would be killed, he rushed out without waiting
for anything and reached the Common soon after the
fight began. Seeing them struggling together so
fiercely, he called out : " You two heroes, please wait
a little while. I am Sogoro and can settle this matter
directly. Please put up your swords." In the pause
that followed, he rushed in between them and forced
them to sheathe their swords. The three then sat
down together on the grass. Wishing to give their

anger a little time to cool, Sogoro took out a gourd and gave them some water. He then said : " Mr. Jusaburo, I approved of your letter stating the cause of your quarrel ; but you must bear in mind that if you are killed now, you will fail in the duty you owe your parents, even though your noble heart may be satisfied. Sad indeed would it be for them if Mr. Takasu were to kill you, their only son." At these words both men awoke as from a dream and felt quite ashamed of themselves. Sogoro continued : " Mr. Jusaburo, it is right you should feel troubled ; but I can tell you a way out of the difficulty. Mr. Takasu and I are united in the bond of brotherhood, and there is no reason why we should quarrel now. You have no doubt heard of Mr. Rokuemon of Takizawa. He comes of a very good family and has a daughter, named Oaki who is every bit as beautiful as Oran and has all her lady-like accomplishments too. It was almost settled that she should marry Mr. Takasu, but now I will get her for you if you will kindly ask Oran for Mr. Takasu." Jusaburo seemed greatly impressed and said : " I will do as you propose and see Mr. Todayu ; and, though I feel myself quite unworthy, will make Oran my younger sister and marry her to Mr. Takasu." The three men felt quite at ease, and after fixing the time of their next meeting, they separated. Truly when hearts unite, even those who have been before the greatest enemies become as brothers. Sogoro went the next day to Takizawa and told Rokuemon just how matters stood, and concluded by asking his daughter Oaki as Jusaburo's wife. Rokuemon and Sogoro were old friends, and so everything was soon settled, and the young people were married at once. In the meantime Jusaburo had explained matters to Todayu, and had arranged everything there, so that Oran was married to Takasu.   All in the neighbourhood were much pleased with both marriages, and were loud in praising Sogoro for the happy way, in which he had settled a very difficult matter; and they felt that the tact and wisdom he had shown, were worth more than a thousand pieces of silver.

CHAPTER VI.

SOGORO MEETS A YOUNG WOMAN AMONG THE HILLS.

At the town of Narita, in the Province of Shimosa, there stands a temple to the god Fudo, the Motionless One.   For many years the image was in Kyoto, but when Masakado rose in insurrection, it was removed to Narita for safety, and many were the earnest prayers then made to it that he might be defeated. When in answer to these, he was soon after killed and the nation restored to its wonted peace and tranquillity; it was proposed that the god should be taken back to Kyoto. But the noble image stood immovable as a rock, without offering to stir, and so at last a humble thatched temple was built over it. The answers to prayers came so promptly, increased so rapidly, and were so wonderful, that the temple flourished exceedingly, and became widely known.

Year after year, in ever increasing numbers, the eager worshippers resorted to it, and returned to their homes astounded at its grandeur and beauty.

At the time of our history, there dwelt near the temple a famous swordsman ; and to him Sogoro used to go to learn fencing. He was considered his best pupil, and being a strong believer in Fudo, he often stayed after receiving his lesson and spent several hours in worship at the temple. Having done so one day towards the end of autumn, it was after midnight when he started to go home. The night was pitch dark and as he got among the hills it began to rain. That is an uncanny spot to be in alone even in broad daylight as the wind whistles among the pine trees, and makes a terribly ghostly sound. As he groped his way along, he suddenly saw a light in the distance ; and wondering what it could be, peered through the trees, and saw a woman kneeling in prayer. Her long black hair was streaming in the wind, and this and her white dress made her look so much like a ghost, that it was enough to frighten any one : Sogoro however, being a man of great courage and fearless disposition, was not even startled. Concealing himself in the shadow of the trees, he watched her as she went round and round the temple and after bathing in the holy water knelt in worship.

When she had finished and was getting up to go, he called out to her : "Will you not wait a little, and tell me why you come out so late, and all alone too ? " She turned at his voice and said : "Are you a ghost?" "No," he replied, "I am Sogoro of Iwahashi, and was

on my way home from Narita when I noticed a light
here, and thinking it curious, turned aside to see what
it could be, and so have been watching you for the
last few minutes." She replied : "Well, if so, there
is no reason why I should hide anything from you?
I live in the village and am the daughter of one of the
retainers of the former lord of Kumamoto. My father
was considered equal in war to a thousand others and
served with honour under Kyomasa in his expedition
to Corea. On the destruction of the House of Tadahira,
my father, not caring to serve under the new lord, was
forced to leave and so came here. He died soon after,
and my mother brought me up in the midst of her
poverty and grief. Just now she is quite ill, but as we
have nothing put by, I cannot attend to her as I wish.
When I think of our family sorrows, I cannot help
weeping as I nurse her. I am ashamed you should
have seen me, but every night I come here, and pray
the gods to take my life instead of hers."

As she closed she burst into tears, and Sogoro was
so affected by her story that he wept too. On recover-
ing himself he said : "I rejoice to think that there is
such a filial woman in the world. Why should the
gods cast you off? There is a limit though to every
man's life and even kings cannot escape when their
time comes. If however you make yourself ill by
coming out here these cold nights, you will fail in your
duty to your mother, so take this trifle for medicine
and run home quick and nurse her."

With these words, he took a roll of money from
his bosom, and handed it to her. Quite taken by

surprise, she said: "Oh! what an unexpected gift! I shall never forget your kindness as long as I live, but please take it back as I should dread the displeasure of Heaven if I took such a large sum from you, who are not related to me in any way." She showed no signs of wavering so Sogoro replied: "You must not think that this comes from me. Wealth is the property of all under heaven, and is given by the gods and Buddha to those filial children whom they watch over, whenever they see that it is required: of this, both here and in China, there are many instances. If you look, you will find bamboo shoots in the snow and carp under the hard ice; with these you can feed your mother until I come and call on her." So saying, he put the money into her bosom in spite of her remonstrances and went on his way. She watched him until he was out of sight, and then bowed three times and went home filled with new joy and courage.

As he went along, Sogoro thought over all that she had told him and felt it ten thousand pities that such a filial woman should be so straitened by poverty. Feeling he must help her in some way, he prepared various articles of food and went the next day to call on her. As he approached the house, he noticed the eaves all decayed and the grass growing thick round the door, unmistakable signs of the poverty of the inmates. He called out for admittance, and saw as he did so, some one whom he took to be the mother resting covered by a thin quilt. The daughter, who had seen him come, now ran to meet him saying: "Are you the gentleman who was so kind to me last evening? Our house is a

very poor one but please come in." On hearing who
had come, the mother lifted her heavy head from the
pillow and said, while the tears filled her eyes : " My
daughter has told me how she met you last night, and
how kind you were to her. I cannot find words to
express my gratitude, but it did her as much good as
if the gods and Buddha had themselves graciously
appeared to her." Tears always come first in sorrow
and Sogoro was blinded with his now.

As soon as he could speak he said to the mother :
" I deserve no thanks. This is heaven's answer to the
prayers of your filial daughter. I only came to-day to
bring a little token of my regard. Please take it and
in future when you want anything, do not hesitate to
come to me as I shall always be only too glad to help you.
My name is Sogoro and I am the headman of the village
of Iwahashi. In spite of your present reduced circumstances, you belong I know to an illustrious family.
Take courage therefore and take care of yourself ; for the
spring will now soon be here with its opening flowers."
The mother and daughter tried to thank him but could
not speak for their tears of joy. He remained the
whole day trying to comfort them : and when he left,
the daughter saw him to the gate ; and, after again
thanking him warmly for all his kindness, parted from
him with many bows.

After this he called frequently to see them and gave
them numerous presents. No medicine seemed to
help the mother and even her filial daughter's earnest
prayers were powerless to detain her : she continued
to grow weaker and weaker ; till at last, about the

beginning of November, she took her journey along
the way to Hades. Then indeed her daughter Okin
cried to heaven, and lamented kneeling on the ground.
After the funeral Sogoro went to call on her and said :
" Death is the doom of every living thing and none
can escape it." He then handed her the present of
money usually given in such cases to buy incense with.
She thanked him through her tears and said :
" Whenever shall I be able to repay all your repeated
kindnesses ? " She passed the forty days of mourning
entirely in weeping, and thus the year closed.

When the new spring came, it found her still living
alone in her grief, but Sogoro who had by no means
forgotten her, often dropped in as he passed. One day,
after they had talked some time, he said : " It is very
rude of me to say so, but no doubt you often feel very
lonely living all by yourself as you are doing. I am
unmarried and shall be glad to have you come and
manage my household. Will you not become my wife
and let us grow old together?" She replied blushing : " I am very much obliged to you and shall never
forget how kind you were to us while my mother was
living. In return I shall be glad to serve you in any way
I can, but I think it would be wrong for me to become your wife. If however you will take me as a common servant I shall be happy indeed." Sogoro said :
" No, no, not so. You were once, I am sure, a celebrated and distinguished woman, and though you may
hesitate to do so, please yield to my wish and become
my wife." As he seemed set upon it, and she really
liked the idea, they were soon married. She made

him a faithful and virtuous wife, and soon had two
daughters and then some sons ; so that their home life
became happier and happier as the years passed, and
they wanted nothing.

CHAPTER VII.

KANAZAWA TRAVELS THROUGH THE VILLAGES EXTORTING THANK OFFERINGS.

Going too far is as bad as not going far enough.
When, towards the close of January in the 13th year
of Kwanei (March 1636) ; Hotta Kaga no Kami was
about to accompany the Shogun Hidetada to Hades, he
summoned two of his counsellors, Watanabe and Hara
—men famous for their wisdom and goodness—and
gave them each a sword, saying : " My son Kozuke no
Suke is very hasty, but you must try and restrain him.
If he should go into profligate conduct, you must remonstrate with him even at the risk of your lives.
Henceforth you must never leave his side. When
a ruler has five advisers, it is said that his dominions
are secure, so do your best to be faithful." Both of
them felt his kindness deeply, and thanked him with
hearts overflowing with gratitude for the honour thus
conferred upon them. His mind being now at rest, he
summoned his old retainers and gave them his last
directions, and the next day committed suicide.

His son Kozuke no Suke was summoned at once to
take the offices his father had held, and was still further

promoted on account of his father's honourable death. Removing to Yedo, he foolishly left the good old customs of his ancestors, and lived in luxury and pride in the height of extravagance. Watanabe and Hara were both anxious to serve him with increasing fidelity, but as they went to reside with him in the capital; the governors in the country, some of whom were very wicked men, had abundant opportunity to do as they liked.

One of them, Ikeura, who then governed at Sakura as Kozuke no Suke's representative, was a great lover of flattery. Avaricious and extravagant in the extreme, afraid of nobody and detesting all who were honest and straightforward, he made the whole district tremble under the weight of his authority. Nor was Kanazawa, who occupied the position previously held by Hara, one particle better. He always flattered Ikeura; and so these two became extremely friendly, and loved each other as the fishes love water.

One day Ikeura said to him: "If we wish to govern properly, we must make ourselves thoroughly well acquainted with the customs of the rustics. I have noticed that many of the farmers, who were leading men in the district in old days but have since become poor, are now looked down on by their more fortunate neighbours. How is this?" Kanazawa replied: "Farmers say that fields are the farmer's glory and always work hard to add to their number. Those who have the largest number are looked up to, even though they may have been farming for only a short time; while those who lose their fields are despised even though they belong to old families. Thus you see that men are honoured or despised according as they are rich or poor. The rich rise to the top, the poor are forced down lower and lower, until it seems to me that the distance between them is as great as that between heaven and earth." Ikeura said : " If so, we must have great wealth before we can make our power felt over the whole empire. An insurrection has, as you know, just broken out in Amakusa and is spreading fast. The daimyos have all gone to try and put it down, and we shall most likely be ordered to send an army. If we can then raise double the required number of soldiers, how greatly it will redound to our lord's honour ! And what a grand show they will make on the field if they all have first class stores, harness, and weapons ! To do this we must collect money, but as the farmers are sure to try and get off without paying, I have thought of the following plan :—

In the village of Kamio there lives a man called Heishichi. Some years since, while digging a well, he found thirty ryo and took it as his own ; but a man named Sakuzaemon claimed it as his, and a great dispute arose between the two. Our lord's father heard about this and added thirty ryo himself; so each of the men had thirty ryo and went away much pleased. Now I propose that we summon Heishichi, and tell him to return the thirty ryo and twenty ryo more as interest. His lands and fields are very good, and he is quite wealthy and has built himself a beautiful house. This is all really due to his lord's kindness ; so as he is a very straightforward man, he will no doubt show his gratitude by paying readily.

Again, when Yorozuya was living in the castle town, he quarreled with Yonosuke and summoned him before the court. Yorozuya was found guilty and was ordered to adopt Yonosuke's son Yoshimatsu and retire in his favour. In view of this, Yonosuke ought to be only too glad to pay fifty ryo if we tell him to do so.

At the same time, let us decide that all who marry, build houses, or adopt sons, must pay a certain sum in proportion to their property. By so doing, we shall gather mountains of gold and silver, and gain great advantage ; but above all, it will be of great service to our lord. Let us therefore labour body and soul to carry it out.

Much pleased to hear it would be to his advantage, Kanazawa, promised to do his utmost, and the next day summoned Heishichi and ordered him to pay the fifty ryo they had agreed upon. Heishichi was extremely glad when he heard the proposal and said : " I feel very thankful that my lord, notwith-standing my low birth, has graciously requested me to give him some money, thus honouring me above even the headmen of the villages and the others with large incomes. I therefore beg you kindly to allow me to give seventy-five ryo." " You are a wise man, answered Kanazawa, " to make such a request. Some day you will receive a reward. I shall do my best to obtain one for you. But as you were only ordered to give fifty ryo, we must write two notes—one a receipt, the other in the form of a petition." This was done and the money paid. The twenty-five ryo Kanazawa kept for himself, only giving the other fifty to Ikeura who did likewise, so Kozuke no Suke received none.

Now Yoshimatsu, who had succeeded Yorozuya, had since been swindled out of thirty ryo and had also had much illness, so that he had gradually lost all his property ; but nevertheless he went to the Office as soon as he was summoned. Kanazawa seeing him said : " It was entirely due to your lord's favour that you succeeded Yorozuya, and are now living in abundance ; so to show your gratitude, you must pay fifty ryo. I make this proposition as just now he is wanting money ; but please bear in mind that you are not the only one asked ; for all who marry or adopt sons have to give in proportion to their property." Yoshimatsu replied : " It was, as you say, all owing to my lord's favour that I succeeded Yorozuya, and I am very thankful indeed to have an opportunity of requiting his goodness even in a small degree. I should be only too glad to give the sum you propose had I not met with a succession of troubles, so that I am now in great distress and quite unable to make it up. I will however give thirty ryo and hope you will kindly accept that." As Yoshimatsu was so courteous, Kanazawa had no alternative but to accept his proposal, so the thirty ryo was paid at once, and the other twenty was left over till the following March.

Ikeura was much pleased to hear from Kanazawa how well their plan had succeeded, and talked with him over further measures for extorting money, not caring how unmerciful they were. After they had had many secret conferences, word was sent round to each of the villages in the district that Kanazawa would be coming. How anxiously then did all the farmers await his arrival! And how they wondered what had happened! At last he set out in state, taking with him two inferior officers, named Muramatsu and Mitsuhashi. He chose the best places for his head quarters, fixing them simply to suit his own convenience. From these he summoned the officials of five or six villages, and asked them how many houses had been built in their respective villages during the last three years, and how many people had married or adopted sons. They replied that one house had been built and five people had married, or that no houses had been built but that six people had adopted sons, just as the case might be in each particular place. Muramatsu wrote down the names of all who had built houses, adopted sons or married, with the property belonging to each and the number of their household; stating how many men and women servants they employed, and how many oxen and horses they owned. He then said :—

"As Heishichi of Kamio has built himself a grand house, and thus viciously departed from his proper position, forgetting that farmers ought to live in thatched houses all their lives, he deserves to be severely punished, but he has been pardoned and, to show his gratitude, has given fifty ryo. Therefore, whoever builds a house anywhere in the district, must give a thank offering; but all must not give the same as he did, but each in proportion to his property, at the rate of $4\frac{3}{10}$ momme to the koku (about 10%)."

"Again, Yonosuke's son Yoshimatsu used to live in the castle town, and was then very poor, but he was adopted by Yorozuya, and thus became a member of a wealthy family : he has therefore given fifty ryo as a thank offering. In like manner any one, who henceforth marries or is adopted, must give money in proportion to his property, at the rate of $1\frac{3}{10}$ momme to the koku (about 3%.) If anybody tries to deceive us, his statements will be compared with the official lists, and the village officials will be held responsible for all mistakes."

The village officials were all much perplexed and held several private consultations, till at last Muramatsu began to fear they would refuse, and so told them sternly that no petition they might present would be listened to. As therefore they could do nothing, all who had built houses, adopted sons or married, gave money as they were ordered, and Kanazawa then went on to the next village and extorted money from there in the same way.

When he had in this way visited fourteen or fifteen villages, he at last reached Upper Iwahashi, and took up his headquarters at the house of our hero, who was now the headman of the village. His full name was Kinouchi Sogoro. He was famous for his wisdom, learning and eloquence; and was so kind and benevolent that he was beloved by all who knew him. Ever ready to help those who were in trouble, he always tried to do his utmost to prevent oppression and be

just to all.   All the farmers, not only in Iwahashi, but
in all the neighbouring villages and hamlets, respected
him highly; and even in those troublous times, all
the members of his household lived in harmony,
working together in peace from morning to night.

Since hearing of Kanazawa's intended visit, Sogoro
had been wondering what was best to do.   At first he
felt inclined to refuse to receive him, but did not well
see how he could : so he tried to think of some way to
find out whether he was really acting under his lord's
orders or not.   He soon saw him coming and went
out at once to welcome him.   Kanazawa asked him
whether any new houses had been built there during
the last three years, and Sogoro told him that Tahei
had built one that spring.   Kanazawa then asked how
much property he had, so Sogoro answered : " He
only has an income of 13 to of rice."   Kanazawa
hearing that said :   " Summon him at once ; " and
when he came, he said to him :   " I hear you built a
house for yourself this spring.   I cannot understand
how you could afford to do so with the income you have,
so I will not tax you like the rest.   You must write a
note for three ryo at once."   Tahei was much embarrassed ; but, seeing the look on Sogoro's face, he bowed
low in assent.   Sogoro thanked Kanazawa and asked
him to let Tahei go, saying he would write the note
for him.   He wrote accordingly as follows :—

To the District Superintendent :—

    For the last twenty years I have lived alone
in great poverty.   At the end of last year my
house was burnt down and I should have

been reduced to extreme misery, had not the
farmers in the village kindly given me trees,
bamboos, and cord; and helped me to build
a small thatched house—twelve feet wide and
eighteen feet long. I have now had the good
fortune to receive a present of three ryo from
my lord towards the expense of building the
above house. I feel truly grateful for this his
great kindness, and beg humbly to present
this note to thank him for his wonderful
benevolence.

　　(Signed)　　TAHEI, farmer of Iwahashi.
　　(do.)　　SOGORO, headman　　do.

Sogoro wrote the above, strongly suspecting that
the officials were not acting under orders from headquarters; but were simply trying to heap up riches for
themselves by extorting such taxes. Kanazawa was
extremely angry when he saw it and reprimanded him
severely, saying: "What do you mean by writing
such nonsense? You have not written at all what I
ordered. You evidently despise me and must be a
thoroughly bad man." Pretending to be much frightened, Sogoro replied: "I am very inexperienced, so
please excuse me if I have written anything rude, and
be so kind as to correct it and let me rewrite it."

At that, Kanazawa became still more angry and
glaring at Sogoro said abusively: "What do you
understand to be the purpose of my visit? If the
farmers become fond of beautiful clothing and houses,
they will not be satisfied unless they have good food
too, and the whole district will be plunged into

poverty. To stop this, the authorities have ordered us to raise these taxes. It was very wrong indeed for Tahei with his small income to build himself a house and it only shows his desire for luxury. For this reason I dealt with him more strictly, and ordered him to pay a fine of three ryo ; but you have worded the note as if he was to receive three ryo. Such conduct cannot be pardoned for a moment. I want no note. Pay the money at once."

Sogoro was not the least afraid but said : " What you have just said is, as I understand it, quite different from what you said before. At first you asked me whether any one in this village had built a house, and I told you that Tahei had built one. You then asked what income he had, and when I told you, you said that it was hard to understand how a man in such a position could build a house, and you told me to call him. I thought you were going to give him some money, as you had heard how poor he was, and knew he must be in great trouble. He used to be the Hira-kawa ferryman and for the last twenty years has lived alone in extreme poverty. He is getting quite feeble now, and it would be monstrous to ask him to pay anything as a thank offering. I therefore thought you could not mean that, but must intend to give him something instead. You should not call me careless for thinking so, for you said yourself you could not tax him like the rest. Perhaps however you wish to fine him, thinking that he has built himself a grand house, although you must have seen from his dress how poor he is. If however you have any doubts about it, I

shall be must happy to take you to see it. You have
been far too hasty. Before ordering him to pay
anything, you should have stopped to inquire into his
circumstances. He will certainly never agree to pay a
single sen of the three ryo. All the birds and animals
have homes in nests or caves; and surely man who is
their master ought to have a home somewhere too.
When a man's house is burnt down, he certainly
ought to be allowed to build a new one. In my
position as tax-collector in this large district it was, I
maintain, my duty to write the note as I did. Receiving and paying are as different as heaven and
earth; and had I made the mistake you say I did,
all the other officials would laugh at me. It is
impossible to undo the harm your coming here has
already done, and I certainly cannot consent to your
visiting any more of the villages if you intend to continue extorting such taxes. It is my firm conviction
that they should not be paid, but in any case you
should have consulted me about them before coming.
You had better go home at once."

Sogoro spoke with no sign of hesitancy and his
eloquence flowed like a river, but Kanazawa thought
his words were vile, and hated him exceedingly and
felt very angry with him. He could however do nothing and so remained silent, and it was ten thousand
pities to see how he blushed with shame. Seeing his
confusion, Mitsuhashi turned to Sogoro and said:
" Your proposal seems very reasonable, but if we go
back now, our superiors will want to know why we
did not visit all the villages. If we say it was because

you objected, it will bring you into trouble, so I think
the best way for all concerned, is for us to take this
note you have written about Tahei, and visit the rest
of the villages without delay."

Sogoro answered : "It would not only be very
difficult for you to continue your visits ; but it would
not do for me to let you keep that note, which states
how much obliged Tahei feels for your present, when
all the time he has not received it, but has only heard
that you intend giving him something. His house is
already finished, and so it is not really necessary for
you to give him anything ; and as you say you have
been ordered by the authorities to visit the villages, I
cannot consent offhand to your giving him anything.
In the rest of the villages, there are probably seven or
eight people who have built houses ; and, say thirty
who have either married or adopted sons : and so you
see what you promise to give Tahei, bears no proportion at all to the amount you will extort from them.
In fine, I disapprove altogether of your visiting any
more of the villages and hope you will go home at
once."

By this time Kanazawa had become very angry and
now roared out : "How high you hold your head
and how insolently you talk about things that do not
concern you ! Mr. Hara must have been mad to have
made such a blockhead as you headman ! I am superintendent here and will not have it said that I was
stopped by such a fellow as you ! Muramatsu, call
the servants and make ready to start at once !" On that,
Sogoro ran out and told the coolies that the visits to

the villages had been given up. The farmers were all
much excited and had clubs ready to knock Kanazawa
down. Had they had a chance how glad they would
have been to use them! Seeing this, Mitsuhashi
went to him and said : " Your visit is exciting the
people and may lead to an insurrection, in which case
the minister would have to commit harakiri and you
would find yourself in a pretty fix. The best way is
for you to give up visiting the villages." Seeing there
was nothing else to be done, Kanazawa consented
reluctantly and went home, calling out as he started :
" Sogoro, you shall repent of this."

Notice of his coming had been sent to the other
villages, and the people there were expecting him and
were much excited. When they heard how he had gone
home from Iwahashi, their joy was indeed great ; and
all those among them who had married, built houses,
or adopted sons brought money to Sogoro for him to
give to Tahei. He refused it at first but finally decided
to take it. In this way altogether he received fifteen
ryo which he handed to Tahei, who was much pleased
to have so much and thanked him warmly. This
Tahei was the grandson of the ferryman, who is mentioned in a preceding chapter in connection with the
quarrel between Sogoro's grandfather and the potatoe
seller.

CHAPTER VIII.

Denzo Made Horse Inspector.

Kanazawa went home highly exasperated with Sogoro for the way he had acted, and lost no time in telling the governor the whole story. Ikeura was greatly annoyed and hated Sogoro more than ever. Glad indeed would he have been to pay him out; but though he racked his brains for several days, he could think of no way of doing so, and so with much reluctance he at last decided to let him be.

Now there was living at this time a man named Denzo, a great intriguer and flatterer. Ikeura liked him well and made him one of his attendants; but he quarreled so often with his companions, and gave so much trouble that at length he had to be dismissed. Being disinherited by his parents soon afterwards for drinking and gambling; he had no means of living, and so became a horse-dealer and wandered about from place to place. Naturally very smart, he soon became well known through the country, and made a large amount of money; but his habits were so luxurious that he squandered it all as fast as he received it, and thus was always in want.

One day he bought some presents and went to Sakura to call on his old master Ikeura, and told him how he had been supporting himself for the last five or six years and added: "I know it is not considered at

all a respectable occupation, but what difference does
that make seeing I can make a good living by it? So
many horses have been stolen lately that owners feel
themselves very insecure; but if you will give me the
register, appoint me horse-inspector, and let me make
every one who buys or exchanges a horse pay a tax;
I will try and find the missing horses, and will also do
my utmost to put a stop to the stealing." Ikeura as
usual was just longing for money, so he was greatly
pleased with the idea and asked. "How much would
such a tax yield in the year?" Denzo replied: "If
in a district yielding 100 koku, only three horses are
bought a year; the district under your control will
yield at least 180 ryo annually." Thinking it a good
way of raising money, and intending to keep it all
for his own use; Ikeura told Denzo to try it privately
for two or three years, and at once had a register made
with the words "SAKURA OFFICE" on the cover and
the Office Seal below. This he gave to Denzo and
told him to show it as his authority, in case anyone
disputed his right to collect the tax. Denzo now felt
quite set up; but what was his delight, when on
examining the Register, he saw that it contained full
information about every horse in the district!

After waiting a few days to mature his plans, he
started out and began collecting the new taxes. Then
indeed were the headmen and farmers all greatly
troubled, and knew not at first what to do; but, remembering how Sogoro had stopped Kanazawa, and
thus saved several villages from paying anything;
they at last decided to go and consult him. Seven or

eight of them therefore went to his house, and told him about the new tax.

After hearing their story, Sogoro said : "I cannot speak positively but it looks very much like a swindle. If it is a tax imposed by the Sakura Office, the head-men should have been summoned and ordered to collect it. I cannot tell why the work should have been entrusted to this Denzo. Any way he is sure to be here before long to try and get it out of me ; and when I refuse to pay, as I shall do; he will be vexed and abuse me. I shall then bind him and take him to the Office and see whether he has not a false register. As he has the Office seal, and has gone about so publicly, the truth will then be known at once. Any way we never agreed to pay such a tax, and no one can blame us for refusing to pay it till we know more about it. Don't be anxious, but go home and tell everyone that I have just bought a fine new horse." Greatly cheered to hear him speak so hopefully, they went home feeling sure that their troubles would soon be over.

Good laws are difficult to devise, but when made bring great happiness and prosperity to a country ; while bad laws, although easy to make, only bring misery and trouble : and so, though Denzo little thought it, his wicked deeds were sure to ruin him sooner or later, however well he might succeed at first. Hearing the talk about Sogoro's new horse, he thought to himself : "How I should like to go and see him at once ! What a courageous man he must be to have stopped Kanazawa as he did ! Before I can hope to tackle him successfully, I must show the farmers how

strong I am, and must also thoroughly ingratiate myself with Ikeura and Kanazawa."

With these thoughts he went to Iwatomi, and took
from there a horse belonging to a farmer, named
Genzo, putting it in the stable of a wealthy man, who
lived at Amatsubo, in the province of Kazusa. The
horse he found there, he left in a stable at Daikata,
belonging to a man by the name of Shoemon and
took his horse, and put it in the stable he had taken
the first horse from. In this way he made changes
in three different places. Genzo of Iwatomi, getting
up one morning and going to his stable, found it
empty; and, concluding at once that his horse had
been stolen, lost no time in telling the headman of
the village. From him he heard of the new regulations about the buying, selling, and exchanging of
oxen and horses, and that three momme in silver had
to be paid on every one ; and was advised to look for
his horse for two or three days before taking other
steps. The next three days therefore he spent making
inquiries in the neighbourhood ; but could hear nothing till the third day when, coming in late, he found
a strange horse in his stable. He at once hastened to
inform the headman, who thought it very mysterious
and immediately sent a complaint to the Sakura Office.

Denzo heard a complaint had come in, and went
straight to Ikeura, and asked him what he should do.
Ikeura told him to send round word at once to all the
horse-dealers in the district, and make them all do
their utmost to find the horse and return it to Genzo.
Denzo promised to do this, but went instead to Genzo's

house and said : " You have I hear, sent word to the Office that you have lost your horse, and I have been ordered to send out bills to all the horse-dealers in the country telling them to look for it, and so shall want three ryo from you for my expenses." Genzo, knowing he could do nothing else, paid the money. Denzo took it and went off to Amatsubo, to the house of the man, from whom he had taken the horse a few days before.

After standing a little while at the stable-door looking at the horses, he went in and said to the owner : " I am the Sakura horse-inspector, and hearing a day or two since that a horse had been stolen in this neighbourhood and another put in its place, I made enquiries and found that Genzo of Iwatomi had had his horse stolen. Here in the register you see how it is stated, that his horse was chestnut-coloured and so many hands high, just like the horse in your stable there. No doubt a thief stole it, but why he should leave another in its place, I cannot understand ; doubtless however you can explain it as the horse is there."

The owner said : " I can tell you nothing except that the change was made at night while I was asleep. When I got up the next morning and found my horse gone and a strange one in its place, I thought it very odd and at once went and told the headman of the village. He advised me to look about in the neighbourhood for a day or two, as he said he felt sure my horse could not have strayed far."

Denzo said : " You are only making it worse by your obstinacy. Many years ago there was a man,

who left his own horse out on a moor one day, and
stole a fine young one and put it in his stable.
Oh! what a famous row there was, and how it was
talked of! You however say that you have had a
cheap horse stolen, and this good one left in its place.
What nonsense! No one but a drunken horse-stealer
or one bewitched by foxes would do that! The farmers
may swallow your story, but the judges will not be
fooled so easily. You will be surprised how soon the
truth will be found out. How comfortable you will feel
then!" The owner trembled with fear and could not
answer. Seeing his advantage, Denzo said: "I
think I can quiet Mr. Genzo if you will return his
horse. If you will also give me three ryo for my
expenses, I will do my utmost to hush the whole
matter up, and will also try and find the horse you
say you have lost." Well pleased with this proposal,
the owner paid the three ryo without hesitation.

Denzo thereupon took the horse, and after sending
it back to Genzo, went on to Mr. Shoemon's house at
Daikata, and said: "I am the Sakura horse-inspector,
and have called to see you about a horse that was
stolen a few days since from the village of Amatsubo.
That horse there looks very much like it. Where did
you get it?" Shoemon replied: "It was put in my
stable at night and my own horse was taken away."
Denzo hearing that, said: "That's very strange. A
person stealing a horse would hardly take the trouble
to put another in its place; however, how much was
your horse worth?" Shoemon said: "About four
and a half or perhaps five ryo." Hearing that,

Denzo said: "That looks bad. This horse is worth nine or ten ryo at least. No one in his senses would steal a cheap horse, and put a valuable one in its place. We will soon show the world how horse-stealers are treated in Amatsubo. If it is found in your possession, you will be condemned at once, and that will be ten thousand pities for you ; but I could perhaps settle the whole thing if I were not so wretchedly poor." As he said that, he scratched his head ; and Shoemon felt a little more hopeful, and implored him to help him if he possibly could. Denzo said : " I should dearly like to help you, but the only way to do so is to stop the petition which has gone to Yedo, and that is very difficult and cannot be done without money. If however you can give me three ryo for my travelling expenses, and will send back the horse you have taken ; I will do what I can, and will also try and find your own horse." Shoemon thought he was escaping no end of trouble, and gladly paid the three ryo, and sent the horse back to Amatsubo at once. Taking the money, Denzo went to Iwatomi and sent Shoemon the horse Genzo had, and thus settled everything. He had got nine ryo by swindling and felt quite proud of himself. Fortunately such audacity, boldness, and cunning are not often met with !

CHAPTER IX.

DENZO STEALS MATSUSUKE'S HORSE, AND HAS HIM ARRESTED.

Now in the town of Chiba, there lived a man, named Mâtsusuke, who made his living by letting out pack-horses. He was very skilful in managing wild horses, and had one which he had bought from Denzo, which was so wild that the people called it, "The Little Chestnut-coloured Demon." Now, as Denzo was hurrying about day and night extort-ing money, but never satisfied; like a man who never forgets the river where he has once caught carp; his eye fell on this horse, and he thought to himself: "I will take it and put it in a strange stable, and then go and tell the owner of the stable, it belongs to Matsusuke, and ask how it came into his possession, and threaten to have him punished for stealing it. In this way I can perhaps manage to make five ryo." So thinking, he took the horse out of Matsusuke's stable and put it into an empty stable at Goimura in Kâzusa, belonging to a man named Shimbei.

Shimbei, seeing a strange horse in his stable, went to look at it: but it became excited; and, seizing him by the shoulder, dragged him into its stall, and would have killed him had not his servants run to his assist-ance. As it was, his shoulder was so badly torn and bitten that it took more than three months to heal.

The horse always pranced and kicked furiously whenever the servants went to feed it; so by degrees, they stopped giving it anything but grass, which they threw into its stable from a safe distance. Living in this way, it quickly lost flesh and became wilder and wilder, until at last Shimbei determined to get rid of it, and put up a notice that he would give it away.

Hearing of Shimbei's offer, Matsusuke, who had now missed his own horse for nearly three weeks, went to Goimura thinking the horse that was to be given away might possibly be the one he had lost so long. On looking into the stable, what was his surprise to see it really was his own horse! Thinking he should gain possession of it more easily if he said nothing about its really belonging to him, he simply told the master of the house who he was, and that he had heard there was a horse to be given away and had come to see it. Shimbei said : " A little while since some one left a horse in my stable one night. It was so wild that it bit me when I went the next morning to look at it, and you see the wound is not well yet. If you wish to have it, I will give it you and will pay you fifty sen towards its feed. Its owner must have left it here because he was tired of it ; but it may have been stolen, and if so, he may come later on to look for it, so if you take it please give me a receipt." This put Matsusuke in a difficulty as he did not know how to write, and was ashamed to acknowledge his ignorance ; but he tried to get out of it by saying he had not brought his seal. Shimbei said, " That does not matter at all ; the receipt will do just as well without."

Still more embarrassed, Matsusuke asked to be allowed to try the horse, and they went to the stable together.

As soon as it caught sight of Matsusuke, it became quiet and allowed him to lead it out without making any resistance. The villagers had seen him come and had crowded together round the gate, saying : "Ah! he has come for the wild horse ! What a man he is ! However good he may be at managing horses, it is dangerous work for him to try and tackle such a brute !" Not seeming to notice them, Matsusuke stroked the horse's back. The people stood round, wondering whether he would dare to ride without either saddle or whip, when all at once he jumped on and galloped off like a swallow. They were all dumbfounded to see him ride so well, but Shimbei resolved to find out more about him, and the next day gave some money to one of his servants, and sent him to Chiba to enquire.

Now it chanced that Denzo had started out that morning intending to extort some money from Shimbei, but on the way called on Matsusuke to ask about his horse. On reaching the house, imagine his surprise to see it in the stable. When asked whether it had not been stolen, Matsusuke said : " Yes : it was, and the thief left it in a stable in Goimura belonging to a Mr. Shimbei. He, being badly bitten, was in such a fright that he was only too glad to give it away. I got it from him without even saying it was mine." Denzo said : " You are a silly to take back a horse that had been stolen from you without saying it was yours and asking how it had got into his stable. You could not have acted more foolishly. You have taken

it without investigation, and in so doing have committed a great crime."

As they were talking, Shimbei's servant came in and
said to Matsusuke : "I am so sorry I did not have the
pleasure of speaking to you when you were in Goimura
yesterday. My name is Kumazo. I have brought
the money Mr. Shimbei promised you and shall be
glad to have the receipt for the horse he gave you."
Matsusuke replied that he would be glad to give the
receipt but could not take the money.

Denzo had stayed in the room and now broke in
saying : "Oh ! You are Mr. Shimbei's servant, are
you ? I am the new horse-inspector. I hear your
master has given a horse to Mr. Matsusuke. Some
time since I sold the very same one to him, but some
one stole it and put it into your master's stable ; and I
cannot understand either why he should give it away,
or why Mr. Matsusuke should have taken it without
saying it was his. It must be looked into. In the
meantime, your master must keep the horse, and I will
take charge of that money until the thief is found."
With these words, he snatched the silver from Kumazo
and put it in his bosom.

Kumazo became very angry at that, and said :
"What kind of a man are you ? Even if you are the
Sakura horse-inspector, you have no business meddling
here. If it is your business to catch horse-stealers, keep
to that. You have no right to that money. My master
told me to give it to Mr. Matsusuke, and I have not the
face to go home and tell him you have taken it. If you
do not give it up instantly, I shall have to make you."

At that, Denzo burst out in a mocking laugh and replied : " Lift your little finger if you dare. Did you never hear of me before? Do you not know that I am at the head of all the horse-dealers, and could if I chose trample on every one in this neighbourhood? This money would not be safe with either of you, so I will keep it. To tell you the truth, perhaps your master stole the horse, but found it so wild that he was forced to give it away. Matsusuke's conduct looks suspicious too, for perhaps he was tired of it and put it in your master's stable to frighten him, and make him pay him something to take it away."

Matsusuke said : " My horse is not meant for riding on. Indeed, beside you and me, no one in this neighbourhood has ever used it, so what could I hope to gain by putting it in anybody else's stable? By suggesting such a thing, you lay yourself open to suspicion. If we are tried, you will have to be tried too, and then the thief will soon be found." Denzo got very angry at that, and so the dispute became hotter and hotter.

The villagers and farmers, hearing what was going on, left their work and ran to help Matsusuke. Several of them took part in the dispute, and it seemed almost settled, when all at once Denzo began using such violent and abusive language that all the villagers said he was drunk and three or four of them seized him by the nape of the neck. Dragging him out of the house with kicks and blows, they took the money he had taken from Kumazo out of his pocket-book, saying they would send it back to its owner for him.

Then putting the pocket-book back in his bosom, they began beating him more furiously even than before. Finding this far from pleasant, Denzo, as soon as he saw an opportunity, ran sneaking off, threatening what he would do to them all, but especially to Matsusuke. Going straight to Ikeura, he at once entered a complaint.

In the meantime, the young men sent Kumazo the money they had taken from Denzo; but he refused it, knowing how displeased his master would be if he took it after being ordered so positively to give it to Matsusuke. It was then sent to Matsusuke, but he refused it so decidedly, that at last Kumazo took it; and going to Matsusuke, with great difficulty persuaded him to take it to buy some wine for the young men, who had helped them.

The following day, four foot-soldiers arrived; and, amid much excitement, arrested Matsusuke. The village officials met at once to consider the matter; but, not knowing the facts of the case, were unable for some time to come to any decision. Fortunately, however, the young men, who had attacked Denzo, went to Chuzo's house and told him all about the dispute. On hearing that, the officials said: "From what you say, it is clear that Denzo was angry and felt himself in such danger that he determined to save himself by arresting Matsusuke at once. If he had been arrested in the ordinary way, his case would have been brought before us first. Our best plan is to write a petition praying that mercy may be shown him. At the same time, he can tell just how it all happened; so that, if the gods graciously lodge in his honest head, he is sure to be set free." They drew up the petition at once and sent it to the Sakura Office but it was refused.

As soon as Matsusuke was brought in, Denzo had gone to Ikeura, saying: "It will not do to try this fellow. That would only disgrace the District and bring discredit on our lord. The best way is just to imprison him till he dies. When he is dead, we can call the officials together and tell them all about his crime and sentence." Ikeura did not care what was done with him, and so let Denzo have his way. Over three weeks went by, but still there was no notice of the trial, and Matsusuke's wife and children were reduced to great want. After thinking the whole matter over, Chuzo wrote the following petition, and sent Matsusuke's wife with it to the yashiki in Yedo.

"I am Miyo, the wife of Matsusuke of Chiba, and beg to inform you that some time ago my husband bought a horse from a man, named Denzo, who last year was made horse-inspector in this District. This horse was stolen by some one on the 20th of July, and was put into a stable at Goimura in Kazusa, belonging to a Mr. Shimbei. He put up a notice saying he wished to give it away, and my husband Matsusuke went to his house and got it. For this, Denzo has had him arrested; and he has now been more than three weeks in prison, without being tried. I have several times sent petitions to the officials; but they have all been refused, and

so I am reluctantly compelled to trouble you.
I shall be most happy to furnish any other
information you may require, though I am but
a woman. Be pleased therefore in your great
mercy to receive this my petition, and have
my husband brought to trial. I send this in
fear and trembling, earnestly beseeching you
to hear me."

The above petition was addressed to Watanabe and
Hara, and was endorsed by the chief men of Chiba.
Put up just like an ordinary letter, Miyo took it to the
gate of the yashiki in Yedo, and delivered it to the
porter, who, thinking it was only a letter, took it at
once to Watanabe's house. He opened it and read it,
and after sending a guide with Miyo to the hotel,
took the letter and showed it to Kozuke no Suke, who
read it through, and then said : "The affairs of
my dominions are all in the hands of the provincial
officials. You had better send the letter to them."
Watanabe did not see what use that would be ; but, not
knowing what was the best course to take, he went to
the house of one of the ministers, named Kojima, and
conferred with him. After talking the matter over,
they concluded that the unjust government of the
officers under Ikeura had provoked the petition ; and
Kojima went, and proposed to Kozuke no Suke, that
an officer should be sent to Sakura to investigate the
matter. Kozuke no Suke was quite willing, and at
once ordered Watanabe and Hara to decide who
should go. After conferring together, they resolved
to send Takamachi, who, though only a young hand,

seemed very capable and intelligent, and would they thought soon settle it. Watanabe therefore explained to him the good and bad points of the provincial officials, showed him the dangers that might arise, and then sent him off.

Matsusuke's wife had received her passport and been ordered to go home at once, so she set out full of thankfulness, and hurrying on to Funabashi, waited there for Takamachi. As she did not know him by sight, she waited till some one came along, whom she thought was him, and then ran out and told him who she was. Takamachi told her it was awkward to talk there in the road, but promised to see her later. On reaching Chuzo's house, he sent for her and asked her why she had made the complaint, and whether she had been directed to do so by the headman. She answered : "Numerous petitions had already been sent to the Sakura Office by the village officials, but they had all been refused. I was very poor, and though I worked incessantly, could not earn enough for food. My aged mother is not strong, and when I saw how she suffered, I could bear it no longer, and determined to go to Yedo and present a petition to Mr. Watanabe. I am extremely grateful to you for having so kindly come, and hope you will do your best for me."

Takamachi, thereupon called Chuzo, and said : " If it is as Miyo has just stated, there must have been some grievous mismanagement on your part. Stealing is a serious crime, and it is monstrous to leave a man accused of such a crime so long untried. Besides, some say that he is really innocent and has been wrongly arrested. The trial must take place early to-morrow, so write out this petition at once, and address it to the Examiner's Office, and add your name and that of the District Officer as the petitioners. Chuzo assented ; and after rewriting it, gave it back to Takamachi, who took it the following day to Sakura, and asked the officials there about it.

Having heard of his coming, Ikeura, coward that he was, stayed at home, pretending to be ill. The other officials had heard indeed of Matsusuke's imprisonment, but knew nothing of Denzo's doings, and so could make nothing of Takamachi's questions. Ikeura was much vexed that he had come and sent him word through Kanazawa, saying : " I am the governor here. There is no reason for you to come all the way from Yedo to superintend this trial. It is my duty to see to it, so you had much better go home at once." Takamachi replied : " The affairs of our lord's dominions are indeed entrusted to you. What is the reason for the long delay there has been in this case ? There has been time already for two or three trials, so I have been sent to take charge of it." Turning to Kanazawa, he then asked him for the particulars about Matsusuke, the Chiba horse-stealer, and on whose accusation he had been arrested. Fearing to incriminate himself or Ikeura if he mentioned Denzo's name, Kanazawa said : " The foot-soldiers arrested him." On that, Takamachi asked for the official papers they had. Kanazawa knew there were none, and so was in a fix how to reply and hung his head.

Takamachi, suspecting he had not got to the bottom
of it, summoned the captain of the foot-soldiers and
the four men who had arrested Matsusuke. When
they arrived, he said to them : " I hear you arrested
a horse-stealer at Chiba recently, named Matsusuke.
On whose accusation was he arrested, or was he taken
simply on suspicion? Was he examined by the Chiba
officials before being brought here? Tell me all about
his arrest, and whether there were any official papers."
The captain replied : " Well, I arrested him by Mr.
Kanazawa's directions and was told to mind and make
no mistake about it as the governor had ordered it
done." Turning to Kanazawa, Takamachi said : " So :
you gave the order, did you? You must have had some
reason for doing so. The trial will take place to-
morrow in the grounds of the prison, and I hope you
will go with me, and advise me how to act."

Kanazawa could hardly collect his thoughts, he was
so perplexed ; but, feeling that his only chance of escape
lay in putting all the blame on Ikeura, he said : " Just
now, when I spoke to the governor, he said that he
thought you had much better go back home. As he
hesitates to arrange for the trial, I can do nothing."
Takamachi said : " No, no, not so. Don't make such
trifling excuses. Is not Matsusuke under your special
jurisdiction? I have come here to attend this trial,
and cannot possibly consent to postpone it simply
because the governor refuses to give me any information as to the rights and wrongs of the case. Remember that it is to take place to-morrow." Kanazawa was silent, thinking it useless to say more ; but

Kanzaki, who was sitting on one side, seeing his difficulty, said : "As Mr. Kanazawa does not wish to act with us, let us take Mr. Ono instead ; and as the trial is to take place to-morrow, let us go home now." On hearing these peaceable words, Kanazawa, fortunately for himself, left the Office without further parley.

CHAPTER X.

Denzo is Banished and Matsusuke Set Free.

When Matsusuke was arrested, nearly all the officials at once concluded he was guilty ; and, not only did they praise Denzo loudly for his skill in catching such a scoundrel ; but they actually refused to rest until they had obtained leave for him to wear a sword. Moreover, Ikeura arranged for him to work under Kanazawa so as to give more authority to his acts ; but though a bat has wings and can fly like a swallow, it can never become a bird : and so, though Denzo wore two swords like a warrior, his character had not improved at all ; but he behaved just as he did when only a horse-dealer. Very proud indeed did he feel of his new honours, and thought that now at any rate, he would find no difficulty in extorting from Sogoro the tax on the horse he was said to have bought. He would thus not only gain some money for himself, but would also curry favour with Kanazawa, who felt, he knew, not a little vexed with Sogoro for having stopped his journey through the villages and would be glad to see him worsted.

With these thoughts, he went at once to Sogoro's house, and began as usual boasting how he had been appointed horse-inspector, and was terribly wild when Sogoro flatly refused to pay him any taxes at all. As they talked, the farmers collected in crowds, becoming more and more excited as time went on. Seeing them, Sogoro glared fiercely at Denzo, and said roughly: " You are certainly an impostor. If you had been sent from the Sakura Office, they would have sent me word first. If this tax is in order, I am the one who should collect it, not you. I will have you arrested." As he said that, the farmers rushed out and seized Denzo's sword and books; and, binding him with a rough rope, dragged him off to Sakura.

That same morning, Takamachi had gone quite early to the Office to see about Matsusuke's trial; but had had to wait some time for the other officials, who came in one by one later. Hardly had he begun conferring with them, when one of them said an accusation had come in from Sogoro of Upper Iwahashi. On enquiry he found that Sogoro had sent word that he had an accusation to make and was coming to the Office. He arrived soon after, and Kanazawa at once asked him what he had come about. He replied : " Some time ago I heard it said that Denzo, the horse-dealer, was going round imposing on the people, and boasting that he had been ordered to raise taxes from all the villages in the district, but I paid no attention to these reports. A few days since however, to my great surprise, I heard that he had been given the Office Seal and Register, and allowed to wear a sword. He came to my house yesterday and tried to extort some money from me, so I seized him and have brought him here, and respectfully ask that he may be tried."

Hearing that, Kanazawa turned pale and waited some time wondering how he could possibly escape from this new difficulty. At last he said : " Matsusuke, who was arrested some time since at Chiba, is to be tried to-day. We are all very busy and cannot now attend to your case; you must take charge of your prisoner yourself for the present." Sogoro was always inclined to be too yielding ; so, though he did not at all like the idea, he said : " If you will give me an order for his imprisonment, I will take him and bring him some other time when you have more leisure. I should however much prefer that you took charge of him as I have no place suitable, and am afraid the farmers will let him escape." Thinking how convenient that would be, Kanazawa said : " You would not be blamed if he did run away." Hearing that, Takamachi, who was sitting by, thought : " That sounds suspicious. Probably this is the way he always acts. As I passed through Chiba, I heard the people talking about this Denzo as if he was one of Kanazawa's followers. If he is, we shall have hard work to find out the truth about the horse-stealing. I will try him first." Turning to Kanazawa, he said : " Mr. Chuzo told me something about this fellow. He has, it seems been going about through the country, extorting taxes on the horses, taking it is said, as much as three momme on each one. Say what you will, horse-dealers are often horse-stealers. Order him taken to the prison at once.

I have made up my mind to try him and Matsusuke together."

At that, the perspiration stood out on Kanazawa's forehead, and he replied : " I will try Denzo myself ; but Matsusuke, whom you are concerned about, must be tried first." Takamachi said : " Are not the two cases connected in some way ? There has been great negligence somewhere or I should not be here. Denzo's case may be very difficult to settle as he has been going about through the country with a forged Office Seal. In any case they must both be tried at the same time, and in the same room." Kanazawa said : " Did not you entrust the whole matter to Mr. Ono, and now you say that they must both be tried in the same room ? " Takamachi replied : " Mr. Ono is to attend to Matsusuke's trial. Denzo's trial is a separate matter. It is quite easy to arrange to have them both in the same room ; you are afraid of something, and are only injuring yourself by your efforts to escape. I will go to Mr. Ono. Send Mr. Sogoro to me."

Sogoro had gone to the Office in ignorance that any petition had been sent to Yedo ; but on seeing Taka- machi, he understood at once that he had come to try Matsusuke. He had arrested Denzo and brought him to the Office, simply to save the farmers having to pay taxes on their horses, and not with any desire of having him punished. But he saw clearly that if Denzo was tried by Takamachi, he would confess everything and would thus bring Ikeura and Kanazawa into trouble as well. As he was racking his brains, trying to devise some way by which all three of them could escape, Takamachi called him, and asked him what Denzo had said, and how he had behaved when he called at his house.

Sogoro replied: "He called to see me about a horse he heard I had bought, and told me to pay him three momme in silver. I could not understand his demand at all, and thought he was imposing on me, as I had never heard of such a tax before. On looking at the Register he had with him, I saw on the front cover the words, "Register of Cattle and Horses"; and on the back cover, "Sakura Office." In addition to this, it was stamped with the great seal, but only the one word "Denzo" was written at the side without any surname. Thinking this looked suspicious, I began questioning him; and while I was doing so, several of the farmers came up, and said: "That is Denzo, the horse-dealer. He spends his time going round the country, cheating people. He is a regular swindler." On considering the matter carefully, I could see no reason why horses should be taxed, as all the farmers use them in order the better to support their families. I therefore arrested him and brought him here as I thought if I did not, he would go on cheating others. I therefore ask you to hand him over to me, and authorize me to issue a notice about him to set the farmers' minds at rest."

Takamachi did not himself care to go into it further than he need for fear of discovering more crimes, and so turned to the other officials and asked what they thought of Sogoro's request. Not knowing how they might themselves fare if it was investigated further, they clenched their hands till the sweat came, and said it was best to leave it to Sogoro. How fortunate it was for them that Sogoro had proposed such a thing! And how wonderfully relieved they all felt when Taka-machi decided to follow his suggestion, and told him to write a proclamation and have it sent out at once! Accordingly he wrote as follows :—

PROCLAMATION.

During the last few months a horse-dealer, named Denzo, has been going about through this District with the Register of Cattle and Horses, extorting a tax of three momme in silver from every one who had bought any horses. He has just been arrested at Upper Iwahashi and has been brought here by Sogoro. If he were brought to trial, he would certainly be severely punished for his crimes ; but at Sogoro's request, he is handed over to him. If however he should ever again venture into this District, he is to be seized and brought to this Office at once.

SAKURA OFFICE.

Takamachi approved of the above proclamation and had it copied and sealed with the Office Seal, and then gave it to Sogoro. As the news spread through the vil-lages, how the eyes of all the farmers glistened with joy ! And how the people did praise Sogoro, not only for the intelligence and bravery he had shown, but also for the way in which he had let both Ikeura and Kanazawa escape and saved even Denzo's life ! That day had all been spent in attending to Sogoro's com-

DENZO BANISHED.

plaint, so Matsusuke's trial was put off till the next, and every one left the Office.

After confiscating Denzo's swords and register, Sogoro showed him the proclamation, and said : "Nobody at the Office seems to know anything about this register that you said they gave you. As soon as I mentioned it, they all said it was forged and were very angry with you. They were just deciding to try you, when I, knowing you would be condemned to death, asked them to hand you over to me; and this, fortunately for you, they at last decided to do. You must go away from here, but you can live wherever you like, so long as you keep out of this District ; and lucky indeed you may think yourself to escape so easily." Almost beside himself with vexation, Denzo ground his teeth, saying : "Ikeura might have told them about me and saved me this disgrace. He has duped me terribly."

Sogoro took no notice of his anger, but calling the town officer and some coolies, told them to take Denzo to the frontier and banish him. Very glad to hear that, they lost no time in setting to work. The children ran after him beating the ground with split bamboos, and some who were fond of fun picked up old horse-shoes and put them on his head for a crown, while others hung rotten mats on his shoulders for a robe. One made him hold an old horse bone in his hand as a sceptre, and another fastened a horse rib curved like a sword to his girdle, and all of them shouted : "What province are you banished to, you poor nobleman? We do feel so sorry for you!" Then they ran home laughing.

The people at the next village had hated him intensely for a long time, and threw stones at him as soon as they saw him coming. As he passed, they also spat in his face ; so that the officials hardly knew what to do, and threatened to arrest them if they did not stop. After this they were less violent, and continued becoming quieter the further he went; but as he reached the frontier and was being unbound, a crowd gathered round, saying : "Do cut off both his arms before you let him go, otherwise he is sure to steal again." The attendants had not a little difficulty in protecting him, but at last they drove the crowd back, and thus enabled him to escape across the frontier.

When Sogoro took the things he had taken from Denzo to the Office, it was seen that the seal on the Register was the proper seal and that the writing on it was Mitsuhashi's. As he was working under Kanazawa, it was clear that Denzo had been employed by Kanazawa. The officials however said nothing, knowing what a row there would be if it was closely investigated.

That morning, Takamachi had gone to the prison with Ono to try Matsusuke. On their asking him if he knew why he had been arrested, he told them about his horse, and added : "Denzo was, I know, very angry at the way he was treated, and that I think is the reason he had me arrested. I therefore beg that he may be summoned and tried." Takamachi replied : " He has already been arrested and banished, so I do not know where he is now." Matsusuke ground his teeth at hearing that, and said : " To think

that he should have kept me in prison all this time,
and now I cannot punish him!" Ono said : "He is
no robber. He has been imposed upon by Denzo. It
is better to hand him over to the Chiba officials for the
present." Takamachi approved of that and summoned
Genzo at once. In reply to their enquiries, he said :
"When Denzo brought back the horse I had lost, he
did not say where he had found it; but only, that the
one in my stable belonged to Mr. Shoemon of Daikata
in Kazusa, and that he would take it back to him if I
paid him three ryo for his expenses."

Hearing that, one of the under officers went at once
to Daikata and learned from Shoemon that, on his paying three ryo his own horse had been brought back,
and he had been told that the one that had been put
in its place belonged to some one in Amatsubo. The
officer therefore went on to Amatsubo, and found that
three ryo had also been extorted from there. Thus he
clearly understood that the horses had been changed
in three different places, and took written declarations
from both places back to the court.

Takamachi and Ono were both much astonished
at his story, and were amazed at the daring acts of
Denzo. Fully convinced now of Matsusuke's innocence, they ordered the Chiba officials to escort him
home. Then summoning the captain of the foot-
soldiers, they ordered him to send the four men who
had arrested Matsusuke to prison for fifty days ; but
he demurred, saying : "They only obeyed Mr. Kanazawa's orders and deserve to be rewarded rather than
punished."

Hearing that, Takamachi turned to Kanazawa, and said : " We have just been informed that you gave the order for Mr. Matsusuke's arrest. On what grounds did you do so ? " Kanazawa broke out into a hot sweat all over and was speechless. Ono urged him to answer, telling him how very impolite it was of him to hesitate as he was doing, so at last he said : " I cannot explain it. I did not give the order on my own authority, but was directed to do so by Mr. Ikeura." " Then go," said Ono, " and ask him about it." As there was no way of escape, Kanazawa rose slowly from the table and went. Greatly surprised was Ikeura to hear that things had taken such a serious turn ! Far too cowardly to show himself, he told Kanazawa to say that he was extremely ill and quite unable to attend to anything.

On hearing that, Takamachi said : " As nothing can be done now, I shall go back to Yedo and come back again as soon as I hear the governor has recovered. You must be confined to your house till my return." These orders he gave, thinking : " Ikeura will be too much afraid ever to let it be known that he has recovered from his present pretended illness ; so, if Kanazawa is kept in confinement till then, neither one of them will be able to trouble the District any more." With these thoughts, he went back to Yedo with an easy mind.

CHAPTER XI.

IKEURA RECOVERS AND GOES TO YEDO, WHERE HE
OBTAINS KOZUKE NO SUKE'S SANCTION
TO THE EXTRA TAXES.

The song says: "It is easier to follow the lion's
head than to blow the flute or beat the drum"; and
so those, who have only light duties, are not usually
troubled with anxiety. Ikeura filled the post of
governor in a large district, and Kanazawa was the
next in authority; yet, as recorded in the last chapter,
Ikeura pretended to be ill, and Kanazawa would not
answer Takamachi's questions, but behaved in a most
unseemly manner. Mitsuhashi, who was working under
Kanazawa, had considerable ability and could have
helped him; but as his advice was not asked, he left
his master to do the best he could.

After the trial, Kanazawa sent for him, and told him
what had taken place, and added: "The writing on the
cover of the Register was yours, and Mr. Takamachi
has taken it with him to Yedo, and intends coming
back as soon as he hears the governor is able to attend
to business. The Governor however dreads his return,
and will most likely resign, but I do not know what
to do. Haven't you a good plan to propose?"

Mitsuhashi clenched his fists, and replied: "What
a silly you are! You have brought all this trouble on

yourself by your stupidity; and now you act like a man, who, on hearing the baby cry, regrets that he had no opportunity of using anything to hasten delivery. Why did you not tell me about this before? If you had only done so, I could have shown you a way out of your difficulty. With what pleasure you must now look forward to the governor's recovery! You girded on your sword this morning with the spirit of a warrior, didn't you?"

Even these words failed to rouse Kanazawa, he was so chicken-hearted. Very unkind indeed did he think it of Mitsuhashi to speak to him as he had done. Indeed, he felt like a man who had gone out to buy some medicine, and had been given a poisonous snake instead. Seeing his downcast looks, Mitsuhashi concluded he was a coward and left him to himself, thinking an attempt to rouse him would be like trying to sound a gong by striking it with a straw.

Going at once to Ikeura's house, he sent in word that he wished to see him privately. Ikeura guessed what he had come about and invited him into his room. Mitsuhashi said: "I have just come from Mr. Kanazawa's house, we have been talking about the position matters are in at present. If he had only told me as soon as Denzo was arrested, this trouble would never have happened. When the governor of a large district like this is so narrow-minded and stupid, and acts so like a coward, he cannot help making a great many blunders. Even though my writing is on the Register, I had nothing at all to do with taxing the horses. I had heard that there were a great many

horse-stealers about ; and so, when Denzo asked for
the Register, I gave it him at once, and told him that
if he acted honestly, I would see that he was allowed
regular rations. There was some delay about this,
however ; and so, being short of money, he doubtless
extorted extra taxes. You had better summon him
and give him his rations, and tell him that he
must not receive any presents whatever from the
farmers. He will be very glad to have the rations, and
the taxes will then be his own idea, and he will of
course have to bear all responsibility arising from them.
If you like, you can also say, that Matsusuke's imprisonment was all his doing, and leave them to settle it
between themselves. If Matsusuke is convicted ; all
you have to say is, that if Denzo acts so selfishly, he
must cease being horse-inspector. You can then stop
his rations and expel him from the District. If you do
this, he can feel no ill-will towards you, and Matsusuke will surely not complain if he is tried and found
innocent. Mr. Sogoro simply wishes to put an end
to the raising of this tax ; and so, if you tell him that
it was all Denzo's doing and has now been stopped,
he will be quite satisfied. We will praise Mr. Takamachi for his skill in conducting the trial, and for the
justice of his decision ; and that will please him very
much, and no blame will fall on any of the other
officials. Such a course would not of course be
honest, but you must confess that it would insure the
safety of all concerned. Your cowardice in putting off
the settlement of this trouble will surely not help
you in the end. I cannot stay and drown with you,

but will escape from this pool of misery to a land of happiness."

Ikeura did not show how much these words pained him, but simply said : " I do not consider the matter so serious, I have been very ill and am sorry to hear that such things have happened but it cannot be helped now. I intend to resign at once and Mr. Kanazawa will have to do the same ; but I think you had much better go away at once, as I should be extremely sorry if you, with all your wisdom and polite accomplishments, were ruined by your connection with this affair. Here are ten ryo, and although it is very little, it will perhaps come in useful towards buying an outfit suitable for your new position ; and I hope you will always let me know whenever you need my help, as I shall be only too glad to do anything I can for you."

Mitsuhashi however refused all his kind offers, saying that he did not need to trouble him. He then went home and fled away with his wife and children that same night. When Ikeura heard of his flight, he laughed in his sleeve, and sent for Kanazawa ; and after telling him about it, said : " Now we must go to the Office and attend to our duties; and tell all the officials that Denzo and Mitsuhashi together plotted the raising of the taxes on the cattle and horses; and the latter, knowing he could not clear himself, has run away. His escaping thus unpunished is all due to Mr. Takama-chi's uncalled for interference—coming here as he did, and attempting to investigate a case, about which he knew absolutely nothing."

The rebellion which had broken out in Amakusa was soon stopped, and the country restored to quiet ; but for some time strict search continued to be made for rebels ; and the great military houses, not only re-doubled their diligence in drilling their cavalry, but also gave money to their retainers for war supplies, so that they might be ready at once in case of emergency.

Now Hotta Kozuke no Suke was just thinking of doing likewise, when Ikeura arrived from the province and asked to see him. Being naturally very proud, he readily believed all Ikeura told him about the tax-ing of the cattle and horses, and the horse-stealing being all Mitsuhashi's doing. When he had finished his story, Kozuke no Suke asked him what he thought about furnishing the retainers with war supplies. At that Ikeura was very glad, and said : "I am but one official, but it seems to me that though the country is now free from war, the rebels are only hiding waiting their opportunity to rise. I do not think you should rest satisfied until your store-houses are filled with money for military supplies, and all your retainers are supplied. Now your father governed so humanely that Heishichi of Kamio and Yoshimatsu of Sakura gave me some time since small sums of money as thank-offerings for his kindness. They were given before your father's death, and so I do not suppose you ever heard of them ; but I now mention them to show you that, if all who build houses, become sons-in-law, or are adopted as sons had to pay a trifle, your treasury would be kept supplied and your retainers would be enabled to go rapidly forward with

their preparations." Kozuke no Suke was not a little
pleased and almost without thought told him to do as
he thought best.

Ikeura went back immediately to Sakura and told
Kanazawa what he had done. Kanazawa's joy knew
no bounds, indeed he felt like another man and lost no
time in again taking up his duties. The two at once
gave orders to the headmen in the District that all those
who built houses, became sons-in-law, or were adopted
as sons must pay taxes. All the money that Ikeura had
before extorted for thank-offerings he had used for
himself; but he now replaced part of it, and sent it to
Kozuke no Suke, who was much pleased to receive it
and thought what a faithful servant Ikeura was. How
sadly he was deceived!

When Ikeura next went to Yedo and Kozuke no
Suke praised him for his faithfulness, he shed hypocrit-
ical tears, and said, " Oh! how unworthy I am to be
honoured with your thanks! To your exceeding
kindness alone is it due that I and in fact all your
retainers are favoured to live in peace. I am ashamed
that you should praise me for such an insignificant
service. The farmers were very thankful to hear of
your great generosity, and have worked their utmost,
hoping to send you some money; but we must remember that bad crops will be coming some time, and
the tenant farmers will then require assistance whatever may be the state of your treasury at the time.
What do you wish to do about this?" Hearing that,
Kozuke no Suke became impatient, and said: " Is not
that your business? You need not trouble me about

that; you have charge of the District. The people must of course be helped in some way or other."

This order was to Ikeura like telling a monkey to climb trees. Much pleased, he hastened back to Sakura, and said to Kanazawa: "As there will probably be a famine some time in the District, and the farmers will then be in great trouble; our lord wishes us now to make preparations to help them, by making them pay larger taxes whenever they have good crops. You must therefore do your utmost to carry out his wishes, not only for his sake, but also for the sake of the farmers themselves." Kanazawa thought it was really their lord's orders; and so carefully considered the matter, and examined into the condition of the fields and lands, belonging to the different villages; but as they were all taxed in proportion to their value, he found it impossible to tax one more without taxing all; so he made a general increase all round, amounting altogether to 14,400 koku, or in other words 36,000 bales of rice. On seeing what a difference it made, Ikeura for the first time really realized the vastness of the District, and said: "I will leave you to do as you think best. If however we give notice of the intended increase, the farmers will raise objections and it will then be hard work to induce them to agree to it; but if we give the order suddenly, just before the taxes have to be collected, the headmen will all be busy and will have no time for consultation and will have to give in. We had better leave it therefore till later.

" We will now arrange for the relevying of the tax, which Denzo began to raise on the cattle and horses. Order the headmen to collect it. It ought to bring in a large amount ; and if we are called to task for raising it, we can say that we did it to obtain money for military stores because the country is in such a disturbed state." Kanazawa being exceedingly avaricious, lost no time in sending the necessary orders to the headmen. He also taxed the spinning and winding wheels that the farmers' daughters used, and the carrying poles ; and he directed that they should be branded every year with a different stamp.

At the busiest time of the year, Kanazawa took the opportunity of levying the increased annual taxes. He made a special register of the amounts due, and sent it to each of the villages, saying that the increase was to be kept to help the poor and feed them when their crops failed. The farmers were in great straits, and wished to confer together ; but as Ikeura had foreseen, they had not time to do so before the taxes had to be paid ; so that year they paid them in full. In addition to this, they were made to do a large amount of forced work for the government ; and so it came to pass that their children when they married nearly always moved to some other district, and thus the neighbourhood became all the time poorer and poorer.

CHAPTER XII.

THE FARMERS ARE DRIVEN TO EXTREMITIES AND PRESENT A PETITION TO IKEURA.

Now there was a farmer, named Sazaemon, living in Shushui, who had three daughters. The eldest had been married three times, but her two first husbands had left her; and the last one had taken her to his native place, as he thought it quite hopeless, on account of the heavy taxes and the large amount of forced labour to try to live with her parents. The second daughter had been married twice, but had both times been deserted in the same way as her sister; and so at last she ran off with another man, and went to live at Ichinomiya in Kazusa.

Knowing how her sisters had fared, the youngest refused to be married, saying that it was no use as she should only be divorced directly, and would thus bring still further dishonour on her family. Hearing this, her father and mother said : "How our conduct in a previous state of existence does hamper us; for though we have had three children, we have no one to look to for support ! "

The daughter replied : " I am not the proper heir of this house and I should be extremely sorry to have to support you in such poverty. You have paid thank-offerings five times now for my two older sisters; but have lost them both, just because we live in a district of such oppression. I have therefore made up my mind to leave and take you both to some other place."

When their two other daughters were divorced, the parents thought it was all because of their poverty; but now, when the youngest spoke as she did, they felt something must be done, and so made up their minds to move to another district. Packing up their things therefore, they set out for Yedo without letting anybody know; but by the time they reached Senju the night had set in, so finding there a hotel with a very kind landlord, they stopped at it. In the middle of the night, a woman near by was taken ill. Sazaemon's wife went to try and help her and was so successful that the family begged her to stay for a month or so. As Sazaemon had nothing special to hurry him, he consented; and so his wife nursed the woman, while her daughter helped in the cooking.

The potatoe seller whom we mentioned in a previous chapter, as having quarreled with Sogoro's grandfather, had settled in the same village many years before this time. Becoming quite rich, he had bought some land and built himself a comfortable house. He had a son named Shoemon, who was as honest and diligent as his father, and so the family lived together in great harmony. But it is said that every one who is born must die some time; so at last the old man died, full of years, and his son Shoemon succeeded him.

At the time of our story, Shoemon's son Shotaro was just eighteen; and he, seeing that Sazaemon's daughter was such a useful woman, made her an offer of marriage. Her parents were much pleased, and after

the wedding, their son-in-law set them up in business.
This answered so well that many of their native towns-
men, calling in on their way to and from the capital
and seeing their prosperity, followed their example
and moved to some district where they could live more
comfortably than in Sakura. In this way, numbers of
houses were left untenanted and a large amount of
land went out of cultivation. Seeing this the headmen
met together and drew up the following petition :—

PETITION FROM THE 186 VILLAGES.

89 villages in the Soma District in this Province.
50   ,,   ,,   Imba   do.
40   ,,   ,,   Chiba   do.
7   ,,   ,,.   Musa District in Kazusa.

The headmen and other officials of the above villages
respectfully present the following petition :—

The tax on first class land, belonging to the
villages mentioned above, has always been
very high, and its collection has invariably
caused great hardship. More than half of the
high land is even worse off than this, and the
same is true of the middle and lower class
lands where the produce is less, and also of
the bad land and mulberry plantations ; while
those who try to cultivate grain of any kind are
all in trouble, whether their land is high, low,
or middle class. During the recent drought,
the people went out and gathered grasses on the
hills for food, and thus kept themselves alive.

In spite of the general poverty however, the
taxes have been increased 24% since last year.

All the people have worked their hardest
and have done their utmost; but as the crops
cannot possibly yield enough to pay the annual taxes, the young men are going away to
other provinces, and working there for farmers, and sending the money they earn back
here to buy rice, so as to enable their families
to pay the taxes. Some one has gone from
nearly every house in the District, and those
who are left behind are mostly either very old
or so crippled as to be quite unable to cultivate their land properly, and thus it is constantly deteriorating; and this compels more
and more to go away. Those who have land
are trying to dispose of it, but no one in the
District is rich enough to buy it, as the people
have exhausted all their means paying the
taxes.

Land, which produced more than 6,000
koku four years since, has deteriorated till now
it only produces 1,000 koku. Large numbers
of people have been reduced to beggary; and
1734 have taken their families and moved to
other provinces : 885 houses have been left to
go to ruin, and eleven temples have been
deserted, and though there are fertile fields
round them, no one will cultivate them.

It is particularly noteworthy that the ones
who have moved away were the best farmers,

and the ones who were the most honest; but
they will come back at once if our prayer is
granted, and the extra taxes and the other compulsory services are done away with ; and this
District will slowly become rich again and will
redound to the praise of our lord.   Being
firmly persuaded of this, we present this petition.

Be graciously pleased in your great mercy
to remit the extra taxes and the other compulsory services ; and then the people great
and small will thank you, and will never forget your mercy.   We humbly prostrate ourselves before you, and beseech you to condescend to consider this our petition, and
graciously to give orders that it may be
granted.

August, 20th. year of Kwanei (1643.)

When they had written out the above petition, five
of the headmen went with it to the Sakura Office, while
the others spread their mats on the ground, and waited
at the outskirts of the town to hear the result.

The five who went to the Office, found Kanzaki there
and handed him the petition.   He took it and after
reading it to the other officials, he said :   " This is not
the first time the farmers have troubled us : they have
been at it ever since the year before last ; so if we let
them go on, there is no saying what the result will be.
In the insurrection in Amakusa, we have had an example of what they can do, and there is no reason why

they should not do the same here. Ants are but small insects; but when they unite together, they can easily destroy even the largest trees: so before the farmers become too excited, it seems to me that it is best to summon their five representatives, and tell them that their petition is granted. What do you all think of this?"

The others however said nothing, but turned to Ikeura, who said: "This tax has been imposed by our lord's orders, received through the District Superintendent; so I do not think it would do for us to grant the petition. When I have a little leisure, I intend going to Yedo again, and will then ascertain how our superiors regard it; till then the petition must be rejected. They are only farmers and can do us no harm."

Kanzaki felt that if it was not attended to, it would prove the beginning of an insurrection; but not liking to oppose Ikeura, he called Kanazawa and asked him to take the petition back to the farmers. Kanazawa thereupon summoned the five representatives to his house; and when they came, stood a while glaring at them with his hand on his sword: then drawing himself up to his full height, he said: "Why have you brought such a foolish petition? It is perfectly ridiculous the way you state that some of the people in this District have been reduced to beggary and have moved away. I will tell you the reason of the increased taxation, it is to make provision beforehand for years of bad crops. All the people will then be starving, and will have no one but their lord to help

them; and so he has ordered us to lay by rice, whenever the crops are good. Do you regard him as your
enemy, simply because he wishes to save you from
trouble hereafter? And you say too that there are
people actually leaving the province. They are dis-
loyal and great criminals to do so, and they bring
great discredit on their family name; so how can they
expect to find any happiness where they go? Their
being reduced to beggary is clearly the direct punishment of Heaven, and in the end they will certainly
become thieves and be beheaded: and yet you say that
they are deserving of pity. In making such a statement you make yourselves sharers in their guilt. To
my idea they must be scoundrels. I certainly feel no
pity for them. Begone instantly with your petition.
I will let you off this time, but if any of you dare to
come here again, I shall have you arrested and thrown
into prison." With these words he flung down the
petition.

The five men had not dreamt of being given such a
reception, and were so surprised that none of them
could say a word. Chuzo, the headman of the Chiba
District, who was with them therefore stepped forward
and said: "I humbly ask you to allow me to say a
few words. Why do you extort money from us to lay
by for years of bad crops, and thus drive so many out of
the District? Your kindness in making provision for
the distant future, does not help us out of our present
difficulties. What an arrangement! Bad crops may
come in the course of nature, but they will never make
us feel ill-will towards our lord. If however we starve

now in consequence of the severity of your regulations, those who are ignorant will become disaffected. This is the point I want you to consider carefully." Kanazawa was extremely angry at that, and said : "What a talkative rascal you are! I will call the guard and have you arrested."

As he looked so threatening, Chuzo and his companions saw it was useless to press the matter further; so they went away, and told the other headmen how they had fared. They decided that it was no use to bother Kanazawa any more, but went at once in a body to Ikeura's house; and, putting the petition on the end of a bamboo about nine feet long, set it up in front of the door and stood round it crying with all their might: "The headmen of the villages in the District are waiting here to present a petition to you. Please open and read it, and graciously condescend to grant our humble request." They cried out thus at the top of their voices for more than two hours, but there was not the least sound in reply from Ikeura's · house.

At last however a young man about twenty, named Kagawa, appeared at the door, and said: "1 hear you have a petition to present, and am very sorry to have given you so much trouble. My master, Mr. Ikeura, said if you had come with a petition, it would not do to turn a deaf ear to you, though seeing it is really Kanazawa's duty as District Superintendent to hear your complaints, we cannot open it here. If however there is anything you wish to say, let Messrs. Heijuro and Hanjuro both come inside and speak for the rest."

As that was just what Hanjuro had been wanting, he at once called out : " I am Hanjuro and am ready to come if you wish. Please lead the way."

As he thus spoke, Chuzo made a sign to him, and said : " How you do joke ! Mr. Hanjuro was taken ill in the street on the way here, and we had to leave him behind. Mr. Heijuro went with us to the Office, but was taken so severely to task by Mr. Kanazawa that he went straight home at once. That man therefore did not speak the truth when he stated that he was Mr. Hanjuro and acted very improperly. We will go now and consult the two you spoke of, and do what we can to induce them to go to the governor's house."

Hanjuro, guessing what was passing in his mind, said : " In the excess of my joy at thinking our petition would be received, I spoke unadvisedly and now withdraw what I said." Heijuro was also standing near, but did not make himself known. As Kagawa did not know either of them by sight, he thought they were not present, and so did not trouble to make further inquiries. In after days they used often to call to mind how Chuzo's quickness had saved them both as from the very mouth of the crocodile.

Kagawa said : " The governor ordered me to bring those two men before him ; but as they are neither of them here, it cannot be helped. Leave this place at once and send your petition here again by the two I have mentioned, after you have talked it over together."

He then started to go inside the door ; but Chuzo caught hold of his sleeve, saying : " Please wait a little. As we are so numerous and have stood in front of the door blocking the way, you must think that we have come prepared to enforce our complaint, but the fact is that the farmers in the District are taxed so heavily that they are unable to exist. Again and again have we sent in petitions, only to have them always rejected ; and as we feel that this cannot go on, we have come to implore you to have pity on us."

As he said this, he presented the petition to him just as it was on the bamboo ; but Kagawa pushed it away, saying : " It is useless. If I received it contrary to the governor's orders, I should be blamed terribly."

" Allow me then to say," continued Chuzo, " that if this matter brings you into trouble, the headmen of the 136 villages will be only too glad to bear the blame. Can you forget how ready the world is to reward the benevolent, and to feel grateful to the virtuous ? Humanity teaches us to spare the life of even an insect ; how much more then should you do what you can to help the scores on scores of people, who are now standing here, earnestly begging for your assistance. We beseech you to reconsider your decision and help us, as we have no one else to look to."

After thinking a little, Kagawa said : " The rations that are given me by my lord are very small, but I suppose they must come in the first place from you farmers ; and so, to abandon you, would be like forgetting the fountain head. I will therefore do what I can to help you but you must not stay here. Go and wait in the town for orders. I know very well that this petition will result in nothing. I only receive it because I cannot bear to see your deep sorrow, but you must

not think I can do anything." As he finished speaking, he went inside the doorway ; and the headmen all
withdrew at once to the town, and there waited to
hear from him.

As for Kagawa, he took the petition and begged
Ikeura to condescend to open and read it. " Why did
you receive that petition ? Send it back to the farmers at once," said Ikeura, almost beside himself with
anger to think that his orders had been disregarded.
" I took it," replied Kagawa, " because I thought that
in so doing, I was showing my loyalty not only to my
country, but also to you, my master ; so please condescend to read it. We can easily return it afterwards if you wish."

Hearing that, Ikeura became still more angry and
said : " I am your master, and yet you do not seem to
think you have acted at all disloyally in disobeying
my orders. It is ridiculous to hear you talk so spe-
ciously about your loyalty, and say you have acted for
the good of the country. How do you imagine that
such conduct can possibly help the country ? "

" Your anger," said Kagawa, " is most just ; but if
you will read this petition, you will understand the
position of affairs in the District." Ikeura however
would not take it, but said : " My ears are open to hear
it if you must read it ; but why should that filthy
petition touch my hands ?" Thereupon without
more ado Kagawa began reading it to him.

When he came to the place where it said that if the
petition was received, the people who had been reduced
to beggary would return ; and that therefore the coun-

try would become richer and richer, and flourish more
and more, he read it over three times and then said:
"That would certainly benefit the country."

Ikeura replied: "Their becoming beggars is all
their own fault. If it is known however that they
became so by going to other provinces; it will be a
warning to others who may be inclined to follow their
example, and thus may benefit the country. What
possible benefit could it be to the country for those
to return, who have disgraced the names of their
ancestors by leaving the District, and have afterwards been reduced to beggary. It is absurd to
say that there would be no more beggars if the extra
taxes were remitted. You surely cannot believe such
nonsense !"

Kagawa said: "It is most important to reduce the
annual tax; for the famous sage said: 'The officer
who lays up treasure for himself wrongs his master,
let us beat the drum and bring him to punishment';
and again, 'Farmers cannot be rich when their lord is
not so; nor can the lord be rich when the farmers are
not so.' Think carefully about the present destitution
of the farmers and remit the extra annual taxes: for
when the foundations of the country are firm, the
country is secure. All the affairs of this large district
are under your control as governor; so be pleased
carefully to consider this matter."

Ikeura was silent for a time, unable, avaricious as he
was, to gainsay the teachings of the sage. At last he
said: "As our lord ordered these taxes to be raised, I
cannot decide about them now; but will try and do

something later.   Now however, the petition must be
sent back."

Utterly disgusted, Kagawa put the petition in his
bosom, and thought to himself as he went out : " From
time immemorial, states have always risen or fallen
according as they benefited or oppressed the people.   I
cannot stay here in such a disturbed place."   Giving
the petition back to the farmers, he left the country.

On seeing their petition returned, the farmers felt
thoroughly disheartened, and conferred together
what to do next.   Hanjuro said: " It is very plain
to me that our petition will never be received here ;
but it has been signed and sealed by the headmen of
the 136 villages, and we have all sworn to lose our lives
rather than give up.   Let us therefore consult Mr.
Sogoro, and then take our petition to the yashiki in
Yedo : it will surely be received there."

The other headmen all approved of this, and so two
of their number went to Sogoro's house, and told him
how they had been to the Sakura Office and then to
Ikeura's house, and how finally they had determined
to go to Yedo, and they added : " If the officials at
the yashiki there will not receive it, we intend to present it to the Shogun; but as we are not familiar with
the customs of the court, we have come to ask you to
go with us and direct us what to do."

Sogoro replied :   " I see it is going to be extremely
difficult to induce the authorities to receive this petition : we shall never succeed unless we are all like
adamant.   I kept quiet just to see what you would do,
and am very thankful indeed that you have decided

not to give in. I shall be glad to go to Yedo with you, but it is no good to start yet : if we go about the middle of November, it will be quite early enough. It will then take the officials the rest of the year to settle this matter ; and as we shall all be away just when we ought to be collecting the taxes, the farmers will escape paying anything this year. Go back now and tell the others to go home, and wait till they hear from me."

When the other headmen heard what Sogoro had said, they all admired his sagacity and insight, and withdrew from the castle town and waited to hear from him.

CHAPTER XIII.

The Petition is Presented in Yedo and Refused.

At the beginning of November, Sogoro sent a notice round to the headmen of the 136 villages, asking them all to be at the Kikiyoya Hotel in Funabashi by the 13th of the month. Accordingly early that morning, they all assembled and waited the whole day for Sogoro. To their great surprise, he did not come, so two of them set out the next morning to go to his house, reaching there the same afternoon. On seeing them, Sogoro said : " I have been quite ill, but am now much better, and hope in two or three days to be able to join you. Go back now to Funabashi, and let all the headmen go together to the yashiki in Yedo, and there stand continually before the door day and night until their petition is received."

The next day therefore which was the 15th, the two men went back to Funabashi, and told the others what Sogoro had said ; and as all approved, they went the next day to Yedo, and arranged to lodge at seven different hotels, twenty of them going to each place.

The following day, meeting near the Kanda Bridge, they fixed their plans. As soon as the hour of the horse (noon) struck, they separated and entered the castle enclosure from three different sides ; and, going to the yashiki in Nishi-no-Maru, occupied all the space in front of the door, and called out in a loud voice, saying : " The headmen of the 136 villages in your dominions have come with a petition, and will feel greatly obliged if you will have pity on them and graciously condescend to receive it."

The gate-keeper was much terrified to see them, and so also were all the other officials. Indeed so alarmed were they, that one of them, named Shinagawa, at once went into Kozuke no Suke's presence, and said : " If we give these farmers time, this will prove to be the beginning of an awkward disturbance ; and in any case, as they have come here inside the castle enclosure, it will injure your reputation, and you will be blamed by the Shogun. I will therefore go out, and try and induce them to go away."

As soon as the headmen caught sight of him, they said : " Look ! Look ! there comes one of the officials. Won't he receive our petition ?" So eager were they that they had great difficulty in restraining themselves. When they had become a little quiet, Shinagawa addressed them as follows : " We are much obliged to you for having troubled to come here with your petition, and we ought to receive it ; but unfortunately our superiors object to our doing so, so we are much troubled. You must all go away from here now and come to-morrow at 11 o'clock to the lower yashiki at Aoyama, and your petition will then be inquired into." As he spoke very kindly, the farmers had nothing to complain of ; and at once to the great relief of the officials returned to their hotels.

After they had gone, Takamachi went to Kozuke no Suke, and said : " As you know, the headmen from Sakura have just been here with a petition. When I was there last year, I found that the Governor and the District Superintendent did not care at all how much the farmers suffered, so it is clear that they have sent this petition because they cannot live. I ask you therefore to send me to Sakura, and give me authority to examine into it minutely ; so that we may arrive at the truth, and find some way of settling it."

" Oh ! that is quite unnecessary," said Kawamura, " it has not come to that yet. To think that such a crowd of silly unlearned farmers should come here in their straw rain-coats, and stand shouting, blocking up the entrance, without minding how much they injure your reputation ! The foolish fellows cannot hurt us if we leave them alone. If they come to-morrow to the lower yashiki, the best thing to do is to send them back to the province."

"Excuse my differing from you," rejoined Taka-machi, " but it does not do to slight even foolish people : for though one green tree may not burn by itself, if several are heaped together, they burn so strongly that it is almost impossible to put them out; and in like manner, even foolish people can cause no end of trouble when a great many of them are united together. When small, difficulties are easily settled ; but if left to grow, they will quickly ruin the strongest country. These farmers may be very ignorant; but they are also very determined, and have provided themselves with straw rain-coats and bags full of boiled rice, to show us that they have fully made up their minds not to give up until their petition is granted, whatever difficulties they may meet with. You had therefore better decide whether to enquire into their petition at the lower yashiki, or send some one to the province to examine into it there. 'You will have to adopt one or other of these plans : for it is no good at all to send them away as they are." He thus exhausted language in vain endeavours to impress his hearers with some idea of the gravity of the situation ; and only gave up and left the Office, when he saw he was producing no effect.

After he had gone, Kawamura said : " If we examine into this matter now, it will be sure to bring trouble to some of us. We had much better leave the provincial officials to settle it themselves." To this, all the others agreed and the following day sent Kawamura's son Kaheiji to the lower yashiki, with sixteen foot-soldiers all armed with sticks.

The headmen had assembled very early in the morning, and when Kaheiji arrived, he found them already standing before the door. He had his clothes tucked up, and did his best to look brave ; but he carefully kept guards at his side all the time, and thus showed how frightened he really was. He said : " As you are all farmers, your petition is doubtless about some local matter, and should have been presented to the District Superintendent or the Governor. You have however come here even to the Official Yashiki ; and have crowded together before the door, without any regard at all to the dishonour your conduct might bring on your lord. You have also greatly annoyed the officials by your most insolent conduct, and by good rights you deserve to be well punished ; but I have been sent here to forgive your crime. You must however leave here at once, you insolent scoundrels."

He thus scolded them, but the headmen remained determined as ever, and said : " Much as you may wish us to do so, we cannot go back as none of the provincial officials will receive our petition. We had therefore no way but to bring it here ; and we shall be extremely thankful if, in your great mercy, you will graciously condescend to receive it. The particulars are all given inside, so please open and read it."

At that, Kaheiji burst out laughing, and said : " Because the provincial officials to whom it relates have refused it, that is no reason at all why we should receive it here, you stupid fellows ! You have broken your bones in vain ; your travelling expenses are all thrown away ! In any case not more than one of you should have come. By coming in such numbers you must have intended to use force, and terrify the officials into agreeing to your petition. It is very difficult however to frighten a warrior, as he is like adamant; so run back at once to your work of cutting rushes and making ropes."

As he finished, he looked all round fiercely and made as though he would go back into the house; but Saburobe, seizing the petition fastened as it was on the end of a split bamboo, pushed it suddenly in front of his face. Completely taken by surprise, Kaheiji started and said : " Do you dare to stop me, you scoundrel ? "

Saburobe replied : " Not so. We have however not the smallest intention of going back to the province until our petition has been received, so please take it and consider it." Kaheiji however ran inside without a word. As there was no help for it, Saburobe set up the petition where it had been before. For several hours all the headmen stayed there, calling out at the top of their voices, but none of the officials ventured to show themselves again ; and so, after waiting till it was quite dark, the headmen took the petition and went back to their hotels.

Sogoro having reached Yedo that day, had taken up his quarters in Iidamachi, and was waiting there to welcome the others. They all went to see him, and told him how they had been trying to get their petition received since the day before ; and asked him how he thought they ought to proceed.

After thinking a while, he said : " I have all along thought it would not be an easy thing to accomplish, however his Lordship Kuse Yamato no Kami, goes quite often to the Shogun's court. Let us present our petition to him some time when he passes. I feel sure he will receive it."

As all approved this proposition, they wrote out a new petition, and on the 26th, hearing his Lordship was to pass, several of their number watched for him. As soon as he came near, they went up and tried to present their petition ; but the people round him pushed it away again and again, and said it was impolite to hinder him with it. Sogoro however managed to go close up, and said : " This is a matter on which depends the welfare of a large number of farmers ; so please excuse my detaining you to present a petition about their troubles. I implore you in your great mercy graciously to condescend to receive it."

Hearing that, Yamato no Kami, moved with compassion, ordered the petition to be received, so one of his attendants took it and handed it to him ; while another asked the farmers where they were staying. They replied, at the Omiya Hotel in Mikawamachi, and then went home.

The other headmen, who were looking on at a distance, were much relieved to see their comrades so successful ; and, after congratulating them, they all went together to the Ryogoku tea-house. Then sending two of their number to the hotels where the others were staying, they summoned them all to the tea-house. As soon as all had assembled, Sogoro said : " Although His Lordship Kuse Yamato no Kami has most kindly received our petition to-day ; we cannot tell at all when the matter will be decided. Under these circumstances, it is quite needless for so many of us to stay here, besides being a great expense. Most of you therefore had better go back home at once, but let five of your number stay here with me. We do not value our lives at all if we can benefit the inhabitants of the 136 villages, so let us do whatever has to be done. The expenses however that we incur, ought to be borne by all; a collection must therefore be made from all who signed the petition, and must be sent us, so that we may not run short." They then had a feast together and separated with many bows.

The next day, the six men, who stayed in Yedo, received a written summons from my lord Kuse Yamato no Kami. They went at once to his house, and were received by two of his officers. " Are you the fellows," said they, " who dared to insult our master the other day by forcing on him your wretched petition, as he was going to the court? Your offence is a most serious one, but it is his will to regard it with special favour. If however, you persist in again annoying him, you will be severely punished."

Bowing very low, Sogoro said : " Please allow me to say a few words. You must not think that this is the first time we have tried to present this petition : we have presented it several times before, but it has been returned each time. The farmers in the villages are taxed so heavily that they are quite unable to make a living ; so as we had no other way and were unable to bear the sight of their terrible sufferings, we pressed forward with our petition, without thinking how much we might be injuring your master's reputation, and we implore you graciously to receive it."

"That is quite impossible, so be quick and take it it away," replied the officers, as they wrote down the names of the six headmen. Seeing no other way to do, Sogoro took back the petition, and he and his companions then returned to their hotel.

CHAPTER XIV.

Sogoro Resolves to Lay Down His Life, and Takes Leave of His Wife and Children.

After the events recorded in the last chapter, Sogoro and his companions felt very anxious, and for a time could see no way of inducing the officials to receive their petition. At last Sogoro said: "I have thought the matter over very carefully, and see clearly that it is well nigh impossible for us to accomplish our purpose. If however we give up now, all the people will suffer terribly from hunger and thirst, and great numbers of them will certainly die lingering deaths from starvation. This I can hardly bear even to think of, much less to see; and I have therefore made up my mind to give my life for them, and appeal direct to the Shogun."

His five companions were unanimous in praising his generosity, and said: "We five have already sworn never to return to our homes if our expectations are

not fulfilled ; but our oath will be broken if you alone
are put to death, and our lives are lengthened out ; so
if we decide to appeal direct, we will all go together
and do it."

Sogoro however was not willing for them to do this,
but said : " At first sight that seems like a generous
decision ; whereas, in reality it would be a very foolish
thing to do.   It is quite enough for one of us to have
to lay down his life, and is not necessary that all six of
us should die.   There is only one petition to present ;
so I will present it, and leave you to lengthen out your
lives."

As he was firm, and did not look as though anything
they could say would move him, they were all silent
for a time, utterly overcome with grief at the thought
of having to part so soon from him whom they loved
so dearly.   Chuzo then stepped forward, and said
through his tears : " Oh ! how generous it is of you to
be so willing to lay down your life ! "

" I can but rejoice," replied Sogoro " that I am able
to do so, and thus help those who are suffering so terribly ; but I should much like to see my wife and
children once more before I die.   If I could do this, I
should have nothing else to trouble me in this world."

Seeing these words sprung from his family affection,
the five men said : " As we quite understand your
feelings, go back secretly to your home and take leave
of your family.   We shall stay here until you return ;
but please be careful of yourself on the way, as we hear
the governor has a great many spies out now, watching
the roads ; and it is said that they wish very much to

catch you as their master hates you intensely and
regards you as the one who originated the petition."

Sogoro, after thanking them for their kindness, took
leave of them all for a short time; and hastened
towards Sakura, pondering as he went along, how he
could best succeed in presenting the petition. All at
once looking up, he saw three children, sitting at the
side of the road with their mother. They wore straw
mats over their rags; but even so, their skins peeped
out in many places. As soon as they saw him, they ran
up, saying: "Excuse our troubling you, but please
be so kind as to assist a poor mother and her children."

Sogoro wept as he thought to himself: "I left four
children at home with my wife; if they should be
banished after my death, they may come to just such
a condition as this." Wiping away his tears, he gave
them a great many coppers. These the children gladly
received, and seeing this, his pity increased and he
thought: "I shall have to suffer death for my fault,
but there is no reason why my wife and children should
die too. If I divorce my wife now, their punishment
will be very slight: I will talk this over with her."

With thoughts like these, he hurried on towards
home, watering the way with his fast falling tears.
Before long the sky clouded over; and the white snow
which could not understand his sorrow began falling,
gently covering up his footprints, and lying so thick
that the road soon became quite white. He thought
to himself: "If I go by the main road, the secret
police will be sure to catch me, so I will go by way of
the Hirakawa Ferry, spending the day on the road and

reaching home in the middle of the night." Fortunately Heaven favoured him ; moreover the snow fell so
fast that all the houses he passed had their doors shut,
and the road was almost deserted.   He pushed on
through the deep snow ; but the days are short in
winter, so that the day soon closed in ; and about sun-
down, the snow began to fall more and more thickly, so
that the standing trees were soon covered with white
caps like cotton ; and the mountains, fields, and villages,
and in fact everything, became white ; so that it looked
like a silver world. Sogoro had been lamenting over the
dark journey he expected to have to take ; and was
therefore very glad of the light of the snow, and
hastened on towards the Ferry which he soon reached.

Now the ferryman Tahei had been regretting that he
had made no return to Sogoro for the great favours,
which both he and his father had received from him.
He had heard of his having gone to Yedo to help the
farmers ; and so, every morning and evening, he bowed
towards Sogoro's house with folded hands.   Sogoro
did not know whether he was in ; and so stopped outside when he reached the house.   Peeping in, he saw
Tahei by the fire, drinking hot wine and trying to warm
himself, talking to himself the while and saying how
weary he was of the world.

Looking round stealthily to see that no one was
about, he called in a low voice : " Mr. Tahei."   He,
hearing some one call him, grunted out : " Whoever
can have ventured to come on such a stormy night as
this ? " Instead of replying, Sogoro opened the straw
door and went in.   Greatly surprised to see him, Tahei

was going to call out, but Sogoro stopped him, saying: "I am on my way home on important business, so please ferry me across." Tahei's eyes filled with tears, and he said: "To think of your coming all this way on such a snowy night, and giving yourself endless trouble and suffering to try and help the farmers! You are like a snowy heron that with feathers all drenched, tries to break the ice, longing to reach the water that it sees below. I am very much obliged to you and thank you ten thousand times." He then asked him about the petition. Looking carefully all round, Sogoro put his mouth to Tahei's ear, and said : " We have had many difficulties to contend with, but at last Heaven has favoured us, and we have received private information from our lord which has raised our hopes. Perhaps you may soon see the day of reform, but be sure not to speak to anyone else about it."

Sogoro spoke as he did because he could not bear to tell him the real truth. Tahei had of course no idea of this, but was filled with rejoicing, and thanked him again and again. They then went out together into the snow.

On coming to the place where the boat usually started from, Sogoro was much surprised to see it was fastened with a chain, and asked Tahei the reason. He replied: "The officials have chained it in that way to prevent people crossing the Ferry without special permission. That however shall not hinder you. I will soon break it loose." With these words, and in spite of all Sogoro could say to stop him, he

TAHEI FREEING THE BOAT.   Page 115.

struck again and again at the chain, and at last succeeded in freeing the boat. They then both stepped
in, and Tahei taking the pole soon sculled them across.

Landing at once, Sogoro told Tahei he should be
back soon and then hurried off, thinking: "I am
almost home now and can be there directly." He
sighed every time he noticed how many of the houses
he passed were unoccupied and going to ruin, and how
the path had gone out of repair through disuse. On
reaching his own house, he stood outside a little while
under the eaves, and looked in. His men and women
servants had all been dismissed, so his wife Okin had
been taking care of her four children single-handed,
and looked much worn : her hair too was all dishevel-
led. Being unable to sleep for anxiety about her
husband, she was sitting up sewing, heaving a great
sigh every few stitches. When Sogoro knocked,
she was quite taken by surprise, but went on with her
work, thinking to herself: "It must be a badger or
something of the kind knocking at my door such a
snowy night, I will let it be." As the knocking continued and became louder and louder all the time, she
at last, guessing who it was, rose, and going to the
door, asked: "Who is there!" "Is that Okin?"
came back in a whisper. Trembling with delight as
she recognized her husband's voice, she drew back the
door quickly and waited for him to enter. Sogoro
shut the door directly he had gone in, and said: "Is
anyone in?" "No," replied Okin, "no one is here
now but our children. Since you went away, there
have been so many spies about that all those who used

to call have given up coming. The ferryman Tahei is
the only one who ever comes round now ; he has been
several times ; but the last few days he has not been,
prevented I suppose by the heavy snow-storm we have
been having. Why did you come back through all this
snow ? It is most delightful to see you, but I am anxious to hear what has brought you back so soon.
But you must be very cold." So saying, she took the
kettle and pouring some hot water into a basin, she
gave it to him to wash his feet with, and then made
him go into one of the rooms.

Though Sogoro had reached home, he was still thinking about the petition, and so his face was unusually sad.
Noticing this, his wife Okin moved close opposite him,
and said : " It seems to me you look very thin, but
as it is so dark I cannot be quite sure, perhaps however
you have something on your mind, if so let me hear it.
The children are all fast asleep and do not know of
your return. How glad they will be when they wake
up ! Every morning when they get up, they ask me
whether you will not be coming back during the day ;
and in the evening they say : " Father will surely
come back to-morrow, won't he, mother ? "

" Our petition," replied he, " has not been received
yet, but we cannot give up, for if we do ; numbers of
people will die of starvation on account of the oppressive government of our lord. Over 1700 people have
already left the country and more than 800 houses are
deserted. The authorities are fearfully angry about
this, and say it is the fault of the village headmen.
Mr. Ikeura has all along hated me very much, and if

he hears that I have come back, he will at once have me put out of the way. As I think therefore that I have no chance of life any way, I intend to present the petition to the Shogun. If I do this, I know that I shall be put to death, and my wife and children will also be endangered. I have therefore come back to-night to give you this letter of divorce. You will thus escape death and be able to support our children, even though you may have to leave this District. At this point, his voice became so hoarse with sorrow that he was quite unable to continue.

Okin had been weeping all the while, but had tried to stifle her sobs by biting her handkerchief. After drying her tears, she said : " You are not the man to listen to a woman's advice; but I am your wife and we have children; and as husband and wife, we are united in both worlds, so it is like cutting a living tree in two to sever this relationship. How could I live after seeing you arrested and condemned to death ? I would far rather be cut to pieces than suffer the far greater pain of having the bonds which unite us severed. It is very kind and thoughtful of you to propose it, but I cannot think of taking the letter of divorce. With you I should be happy anywhere, even among the mountains : so if we cannot continue to live here, we had better take our children and go and hide somewhere. Don't you wish to do this ? " So saying, she wept again.

Sogoro's heart was full as he looked at his wife's face, and he pitied her more and more, but tried to hide his falling tears with his sleeve, and said : " It

would as you say be very easy for us to go away and
hide ourselves somewhere; but all the people of the
136 villages are looking to me for assistance, and if I
leave them now when I have the chance of helping
them and go away and hide myself, they will certainly
point their fingers at me in scorn : whereas, if I take
their place and petition direct and am then put to death,
I shall have the glory the sage referred to when he
said : 'When tigers die, they leave their skins behind ; and in like manner, when men die they should
leave famous names behind them.' It is impossible to
make me change my mind, so don't say any more
about it, but take this letter of divorce and bring up
our four children."

So saying, he took the letter from his bosom and
offered it to his wife; but she pushed it away, saying:
"I have been told that the relation between husband
and wife is for both worlds and not only for this. We
may indeed be condemned to death, but if we meet our
end together, we shall be able to rejoice even in the
midst of our sufferings. In any case however, I have
sworn whatever you may say never to accept that letter
of divorce."

Overcome with admiration at her courage, Sogoro
said : " You are indeed a woman fit to be my wife ;
and so, though we go to the next world, we will not
change our minds nor sever the ties that bind us
together." At that, Okin was very glad in spite
of the sorrow which filled her breast—sorrow indeed too great for the righteous and faithful woman to
bear.

SOGORO TAKING LEAVE OF HIS FAMILY.

Page 119.

Just then, the cocks in all the houses informed them that the morning was coming. Much surprised to find it was so late, Sogoro rose to go, saying: "I came here secretly and must go back before it is light or I shall be seen."

Then indeed could his wife Okin contain her sorrow no longer, but wept so loudly that the noise woke their four children, and Sohei and Gennosuke jumped up and seized hold of their father, saying: "Father has come home!" On that, Kihachi and Rokunosuke, young as they were, were so transported with joy that they seized hold, the one of his father's knees and the other of his neck; and all four of them jumped about, screaming: "Oh! father has come back! Father has come back! What joy we shall have from to-morrow!" Patting them on the back and stroking their heads, Sogoro said: "Be good children and after to-morrow I shall never go away again." His heart however was well nigh bursting with pity and love for his charming children, and he shed tears of blood, and his iron will was weakened by the pain of severing these close ties of affection. His wife Okin, utterly overcome with grief, lay on the ground weeping.

Again across the deep snow came the crowing of the cocks; and Sogoro, knowing he must delay no longer, hurriedly tied on his straw sandals, and with a few last words of exhortation to his wife and loving farewell to his children, started to go; but his children wept loudly and seizing him round the waist, would not let go, saying: "Father where are you going? Please take us with you." At last making a mighty effort, he tore himself away and hurried off towards Yedo.

Now Denzo had not improved at all since he had been banished, but had wandered about through the country adding crime to crime. Being hated by every one, he was left entirely to himself, for the proverb says: ' Wickedness travels a thousand miles'; and so, go where he would, his wickedness was well known. He heard with pleasure how the people in the Sakura District had been reduced to poverty by the cruel government of Ikeura and his associates and had sent a petition to Yedo ; and nodded to himself, thinking : " Now is the time. If I can only manage to catch Sogoro, I am sure to be well rewarded. I will become one of Ikeura's spies." With these thoughts he went to Ikeura, who was very glad indeed to see him, and engaging him at once, sent him to watch the main and private roads between Sakura and Yedo.

As for Sogoro, after parting from his wife and children he hurried on through the snow to the Ferry. There he found Tahei waiting for him and was soon rowed across. Stepping ashore, he took hold of Tahei's hand and raised it for a moment to his head. Much astonished at that, Tahei said : " Sogoro, my master, it is not right for you to do so ! " Overhearing this, Denzo who happened to be just passing, thought: " How lucky I am to find Sogoro here ! Heaven favours me at last. I will arrest him and take him to Sakura." He therefore hid himself in a grove near by, and when Sogoro suspecting no danger came along a few minutes later, he crept up silently through the snow and seized him suddenly from behind. Quickly freeing himself, Sogoro looked to see who had attacked him. Much surprised to find it was Denzo, he at once prepared to defend himself, and said : " Denzo, you exile ! You are an insolent rascal to dare to attack me." Denzo replied : " Though you are a headman and have received great benefits from the authorities, you complain of their oppressive government and have actually made a forcible complaint about the wickedness of your lord, so Mr. Ikeura has ordered me to arrest you. I have therefore been inquiring for you all round and have now found you at last, so come with me : for you cannot escape." With that, he rushed at him in a fury. Sogoro struggled to escape but all at once his foot slipped and he fell down in the snow. Denzo, thinking he had him, pressed him down and took out a rope to bind him.

Now Tahei, after parting with Sogoro, had stayed outside his house watching him, and bowing even after he had gone out of sight. Hearing sounds of quarreling, he seized his pole and rushed to see what was the matter. When he saw that Denzo had Sogoro down and had begun to tie his arms together, he at once lifted his pole and struck Denzo on the head so hard, that his skull was broken, and he fell dead at once without a word. Sogoro was much surprised, and said : " As he was an outlaw, there ought not to be any strict investigation into the circumstances of his death. In case however, Mr. Ikeura had really engaged him and should hear about it, it will bring you into trouble. I have already resolved to petition direct, and cannot but

rejoice to give my life for so many thousands of my
countrymen ; but it would be a great pity if you were
condemned to death on account of this unhappy act.
Escape from this place and hide somewhere for a time.
I will tell Mr. Chuzo and the others about you, and ask
them to help you and am sure they will do so, but you
have no time to lose if you wish to escape. Be quick!
Be quick!" Tahei shook his head, and said : "I am
very much obliged to you for all your kind care, but
please don't trouble yourself about me, as I am worth
no more than a cat or dog. Your life however is of
great importance just now. You had better be quick
and leave here." Sogoro replied : "I will go now
and so must part with you for the last time. I shall
never forget your kindness and hope you will pass the
rest of your life in peace." Then brushing off the
snow that had accumulated on his clothes, he hurried
off towards Yedo.

As Tahei watched him, he said to himself : "Oh, the
benevolence, and bravery, and goodness of Sogoro, the
headman of Iwahashi! To think of his bearing so
much suffering for others ; and now, not content with
this, joyfully preparing to lay down his life to save
them from poverty and hardship! How much have I
been longing for an opportunity to repay him for all
the kindness I and my father have received from him ;
and now at last, I have had the good fortune to come
to his rescue and finish that wretch Denzo! It is no
use for me to live any longer. I had better kill myself before Ikeura hears of his death." He therefore
hung himself with a rope, and sad to say died there.

As soon as the report of this occurence reached the Sakura Office, the officials went to examine into the matter. They saw the two corpses, but could find out nothing further; and so concluding that Tahei had killed Denzo, and then hung himself, they made no further enquiry.

CHAPTER XV.

SOGORO PRESENTS THE PETITION TO THE SHOGUN AND IS CONDEMNED TO DEATH.

On reaching the hotel in Iidamachi, Sogoro, with the help of the other five headmen, wrote out a fresh petition; and then made his preparations for presenting it to the Shogun. Knowing that he always visited Toeizan on the 20th. of the 12th month, they planned to present it to him then. Sogoro asked the others to look after his wife and children after he was gone; and they, admiring his patriotism and courage, willingly consented to do what they could and parted from him with tears of blood, and hearts bursting with sorrow. Not liking however to leave him to carry out alone a service which so nearly concerned them all, they decided to remain in Yedo and see how matters went.

Putting the petition in his bosom, Sogoro started out about 7 o'clock in the morning of the 20th. of the 12th month, in the first year of Shoho (Jan. 7th, 1645); and

hiding himself under the bridge east of Sammaebashi
b·fore one comes to the Kuromon in Ueno, waited for
the Shogun to pass. At length seeing the procession
approaching, he quietly crept out greatly to the astonishment of the attendants. Paying no attention to
them, he advanced to where the Shogun was and presented his petition to him direct. It was received by
the side guards who ordered him away; and he,
delighted at having accomplished his object, tried to
withdraw, but some of the officials ran up and arrested
him : for at that time it was the law that any one who
petitioned direct should be imprisoned.

The complaint which he had presented was received by His Lordship Inoue Kawachi no Kami,
who seeing that Sogoro of Iwahashi, in the District of Sakura, was the petitioner, handed it to His
Lordship Kozuke no Suke, the master of that
District. Kozuke no Suke having received it, went
back to his yashiki and read it. Greatly surprised to
see it had reference to increased rates and taxes about
which he knew nothing, he summoned one of his ministers, named Kojima, and said : "See what the
meaning of this petition is." When Kojima had
finished reading it through, he replied : "As this is
certainly due to the selfishness of the provincial officials
and to their oppression of the farmers, I think the best
way is to send some one to Sakura to make investiga-
tions.", Kozuke no Suke said : "It may be owing to
the harshness of the provincial officials that the farmers
brought their petition to the yashiki in Yedo ; but you
ought to have received and examined into it then, and

thus prevented its becoming known all through the
palace as it is now. It will be almost impossible for
me ever to wipe out the disgrace of this. The increased rates and taxes must, as the farmers request, be
remitted at once and the annual taxes must be collected as they were formerly. As the petition was signed
by all the headmen in the District, Sogoro ought not
to bear all the punishment, though as he petitioned
direct, his offence is much the most serious. We must
have him delivered to us by the government, and then
he and his wife must be crucified at Sakura, his sons
must all be put to death and his house and property
confiscated. Rokurobe, Juroemon, Chuzo, Hanjuro,
and Saburobe, his five companions must be transported.
Mind you attend to this, but pay no attention to the
families and possessions of these last five." " Sogoro's
crime," replied Kojima, " is indeed very great as he was
not only the originator of the petition, but also the one
who presented it; it is reasonable therefore that he
should be crucified ; but his wife was in the province
at the time, and could know nothing about her husband's action. Even if she did, she could not prevent
it, as it was for all the farmers. I fear therefore that it
is not right to condemn them both ; so I beg of you to
show mercy to her and her children." Kozuke no
Suke however was much troubled on account of the
disgrace that had been brought upon him before the
court : moreover he feared the Shogun's displeasure ;
and being naturally very quick tempered, and not
knowing how the matter would end, his face showed
no signs of relenting.

Seeing this, Kojima continued : "His sons are
so young that they could know nothing of their father's
crime. You ought at least to spare their lives."
Kozuke no Suke said : "Even though they are
children, they deserve to die. Their father's offence
was so great. They cannot be allowed to escape."
Kojima continued : "Even though their father's
crime was very great, it seems to me that putting
children to death, who do not know the east from the
west, will not show you as a humane governor ; so I
implore you to spare them." Having thus tried his
utmost, Kojima retired to consider what to do. Remembering all at once that Kozuke no Suke's father
had appointed Watanabe and Hara to advise his son in
such cases, he went and talked the matter over
with them. "Your reasons," replied they, "are much
the same as those our late master would have given,
and if they have not been accepted, it is not likely that
anything we can say will be listened to ; however, we
will try what we can do." They thereupon went into
their master's presence and spoke together, saying :
"As Sogoro has petitioned direct, his offence is great
and you have done quite right in sentencing him to be
crucified ; but as we have heard that his wife and
children have been sentenced to the same punishment,
we have come to ask whether you will not reconsider
their sentence. To say that these youngsters knew
their father was going to present a petition to the
Shogun is nonsense, and to put them to death for their
father's crime would be barbarous and would injure
your reputation more even than Sogoro's action has

done." Kozuke no Suke said : "Although there is
reason in what you say, I cannot consent to spare their
lives. Kiyomori saved Yoshitomo's children, and
afterwards his family was destroyed by them. Again,
Kudo Suketsune spared Ichiman and Hako and then
was killed by them while out hunting. In like manner, if these children grow up, they will not know
what their father's crime was, and so will hate me.
The only safe way in such cases is to destroy the root
and then the leaves will wither away. Say no more
about it." With these words he rose and went
into another room, leaving them looking at each
other in speechless astonishment. After waiting
a few minutes, they withdrew, and as they did so,
Watanabe said to Hara : "Oh what cowardly words
for our master to say ! He ought not to utter such
shameful words even before us. What do you think
of it? The proverb says : 'After remonstrating,
leave the province if your advice is not attended to ';
and I shall do so, as I have no wish to serve under
such a master any longer." He made his preparations
the same night ; and, taking his wife and children, removed to another province. Truly when the wise
men had all died, the Chinese dynasty "In" soon
came to an end, and the thoughtful people of the time
wondered what would happen next.

Many exhausted language remonstrating with Kozuke no Suke about Sogoro's severe punishment, saying that though his offence was indeed great as he had
petitioned direct ; yet it was not right to include his
wife and all his children in the same punishment ; but

Kozuke no Suke had made up his mind that the sentence should be executed on them all and so would not listen. Sogoro was therefore delivered over by the Shogun and sent to Sakura and put in prison.

When Kozuke no Suke next went to court, he consulted his colleagues there, saying : "The other day, one of the farmers in my dominions, named Sogoro, presented a petition to the Shogun; and will of course receive severe punishment for his insolence. There were however five others associated with him, about whose punishment I wish to consult you, as I think you can help me to decide rightly." My lord Yamato no Kami replied : "Though those five were leaders, their crime is not great. Whenever the lower classes are suffering, they naturally appeal to their lord. Of this there have in the past been many instances, and it must always be so. What then is their crime ? Why punish them at all ? However as Sogoro is to be so severely punished, these five men will not be satisfied to be let off with no punishment at all." "Well then," asked Kozuke no Suke, " ought they to be banished ? " Yamato no Kami replied : " It is not necessary to banish them ; but simply forbid them to come within 25 miles either of Yedo or of your dominions. You have already had Sogoro the chief offender delivered over to you, and have decided on his punishment yourself; so you have no right to banish the others to an island, where they would be under the jurisdiction of the Shogun, particularly as they have not offended against his government. Understand that this is my private advice to you and is not given officially." Greatly vexed to be spoken to in such a way, my Lord Kozuke no Suke hardly knew what to do, but finally decided to take his advice.

Thus the year closed, and the following one, the 2nd of Shoho, on the 25th of the 1st month (Feb. 11th 1645), the five headmen were summoned and sentenced as follows :—

You, whose names are given below, are the five scoundrels who led the farmers in their petition and most insolently pressed it on the Minister as he was riding along. You were not however present when Sogoro forced his petition on the Shogun ; so the death penalty is remitted in your cases ; but you are forbidden to come within 25 miles either of Yedo or of the District of Sakura. Your families are unpunished.

Rokurobe, headman of Oda.

Hanjuro	do.	Koizumi.
Chuzo	do.	Chiba.
Juroemon	do.	Lower Kazuta.
Saburobe	do.	Upper Kazuta.

The above sentence was written out at the Office in Yedo, as also that against Sogoro and his family. The two were then intrusted to Shinagawa, one of the inspectors. He made ready and went at once to Sakura with four other officials.

As the provincial officials had not been consulted at all, they were quite in the dark about what had been taking place in Yedo, and felt very uneasy as to what would be the outcome of the visit of these five officials ;

indeed they seemed like men treading on a tiger's tail. Ikeura, knowing that the difficulty had all been caused by his own avarice, and thinking it would be difficult to give a reason for the extra taxes he had been extorting, pretended to be ill just as he had done the previous November and did not go to the Office.

The officials from Yedo arrived at Sakura, and on the 4th of the same month they had Sogoro brought from the prison, and summoned all the headmen of the 136 villages. Inside the Office there were in all forty-six officials, while the 130 headmen stood outside in the spacious courtyard. When all were ready, Takamachi took the petition from his bosom; and opening it, laid it down before him, and addressed the headmen as follows: "I notice you state in your petition that the taxes have been raised 24%. Is this true? Did you really pay that amount?" Heijuro of Lower Iwahashi replied: "It is true." Takamachi then said: "Who ordered you to pay so much? Was it not the District Superintendent?" Heijuro replied: "Mr. Kanazawa, the District Superintendent, gave us each a notice and an examining register; and each of the headmen has the register here that was then given him, so I pray you to look at them." With these words, he took his own from his bosom and handed it to Takamachi, who took it and saw on the front cover the words, "Register of Annual Rates and Taxes," and on the back the names of Muramatsu Jimbei and Mitsuhashi Goheiji. He then took four or five from others and on examining them saw they were all alike. He next asked: "What are the various other taxes you say you were ordered to pay?" Heijuro replied: "Those who built new houses had to pay over four momme in silver on every koku of their income, as also those who adopted sons or married. Again every one who bought a horse or exchanged one had to pay a tax of three momme in silver." On hearing that, Takamachi turned to where the provincial officials were sitting, and said: "This is fearful. The sage indeed spoke the truth when he said, 'It is better to have a robber for an official than an oppressor.' How terrible! How terrible!" At these words, the provincial officials turned pale; and those who had taken part in extorting the unjust taxes, were almost dead with fright. After a long pause, Takamachi turned again to Heijuro and said: "Your petition is granted, and all the extra taxes are remitted. Hereafter you need only pay the same amounts as you did during the period of Kwanei under Oi no Kami." Heijuro replied: "We are greatly obliged to you for your gracious order. As we have not yet paid the taxes for last year, we will pay them at once on the basis you say." "You can do so," replied Takamachi, "taking out the amounts you have already paid for building houses, adopting sons, and marrying, also the duties on horses." On hearing that, all the headmen shed tears of joy, and bowed down to the ground, and did not raise their heads for some time. Though Takamachi had spoken without having consulted the other officials, not one of them raised any objection; so the headmen were dismissed with hearts overflowing with thankfulness.

Then Shinagawa, having ordered Sogoro to be brought out in front of the prison, stood up and read his sentence to him as follows :—

Making yourself leader of the farmers, you pushed yourself forward above the others, and insolently pressed your complaint on His Lordship Kuse Yamato no Kami as he was going to the castle. Not content with this you even had the audacity to force it afterwards on the Shogun himself. For this insolent act, you and your wife are condemned to be crucified, so make your preparations accordingly. Your four sons are to be beheaded.

The following are the persons referred to in the above sentence :—

Sogoro, the headman of Upper Iwahashi aged 49
His wife Okin.................................... do. 38
Their oldest son, Sohei........................ do. 13
Their second son, Gennosuke .... do. 10
Their third son, Kibachi .... do. · 8
Their fourth son, Rokunosuke.............. do. 4

On hearing the sentence on Sogoro, Zembei the headman of the village of Sakato was much troubled and sent a letter round to the villages asking all the headmen to meet him at the temple of Zenshoji in Miroku Cho in the castle town. They met at once wondering what had happened. Zembei said to them : "The success of our last petition is all due to Mr. Sogoro, who willingly sacrificed his life for our good. And now, not only has he to die, but his wife and his four sons are also going to be put to death.

Thus six people are to die for the sake of the 136 villages. Why must we see this? I feel very sorry too for his relatives. How do you all feel about it?" Hanyemon, the headman of the village of Kazuta, advanced and said: "Truly it is not right for us to leave it as it is. What would you all think of our writing another petition, and asking that the lives of his wife and children, five in all may be spared?" To this the headmen of the villages agreed unanimously, saying: "If we had been given the same punishment, we would not have minded." Accordingly Heijuro of Lower Iwahashi at once wrote out a petition which read as follows:—

We most respectfully present the following petition:—

The headmen of the villages and all down to the lowest tenant humbly thank you for your gracious order, remitting the increased taxes and other rates and allowing us to pay the same amount of taxes as we did in the old days. Sogoro the headman of the village of Upper Iwahashi in the Inba District, recently presented a petition to the Shogun. You may have thought that this was his own idea, but that it was not so is proved by its having been signed by all the headmen of the 136 villages. The fact is that none of the other headmen were acquainted with public business; and so we compelled him to be our leader much against his will. We therefore feel much grieved that our conduct has brought him such a heavy punishment. At the same time we know that your sentence on him is most reasonable as he ventured to appeal direct to the Shogun. We are however very sorry for his wife and children, and implore you to show them mercy and hand them over to us. We should all feel very thankful if you would punish us in their stead. Most humbly do we ask you graciously to accept this our petition.

Zembei, the headman of Sakato.

Hanyemon   do.   Kazuta.

Hanjuro   do.   Lower Iwahashi.

representing the 136 villages.

2nd month of the 2nd. year of Shoho (Feb. 1645.)

The petition was written as above and presented at the Sakura Office. Kanzaki took it and after reading it, said : " You have done nobly in offering such a petition ; but I can do nothing in the matter as our lord himself gave the orders. If you wish to try and save the lives of Mr. Sogoro's wife and children, you must go to Yedo with the priest of the temple they belong to and their relations; and present your petition there." Accordingly making ready at once, they hastened to Yedo and presented their petition ; but Kozuke no Suke was very angry and said to them : " Sogoro's act was so audacious that if it had not been for my rank I should have been ruined. I cannot therefore rest contented with crucifying him alone. I will excuse you this time ; but if you come bothering me with any more such petitions, I shall put you all to death as well as his wife and children." As there was thus no help they went home.

On reaching the Sakura Office, they asked to be allowed to take leave of Sogoro before he died; but were told that it could not be permitted. They were however advised to go to the prison officials and see if they could not accomplish it in some way or other. Accordingly they all went to the prison, and humbly asked the officials who replied: "We are sorry to have to refuse to allow you to see Sogoro, but we will allow you to speak to him." The three men therefore went up to the window of his prison and called out: " Mr. Sogoro: we are Hanyemon, Zembei and Heijuro. In regard to your sentence, we have been petitioning that the lives of your wife and children might be spared; but we have been refused and so there is nothing more to be done. The farmers of the 136 villages have however been relieved from their troubles; and as this is all due to your kindness, all of them even to the poorest tenant are mourning your loss, and so you may rest satisfied, as we have charged ourselves with performing mass for your whole family." As they thus spoke, their tears blinded them, and Sogoro had hard work to restrain his feelings while he said : "Even in future ages I shall never forget your great kindness. As I am not being punished for wrong doing, I shall neither be blamed for unfilial conduct towards my ancestors, nor leave behind me a bad name for after ages. My life is given for all the people and so I can only rejoice, in fact it has been my life-long wish so to die. Do not

therefore grieve for me ; but if you happen to think of
these sad days hereafter, I wish you would pray for
me. Please remember me to the others." On hearing these brave words, the three men clung to the
lattice of the prison window, and wept for a little
while in silence. Soon however, one of the guard told
them that their time was up ; and so they said farewell
and went to their homes.

On the 9th. of the 2nd month in the 2nd year of Shoho, (Feb. 22nd 1645), Kanzaki summoned the officials
of Upper Iwahashi, and said : " As the day after to-
morrow, the 11th. is the day fixed for Sogoro's execution, you must deliver his household furniture and all
his implements to his two daughters, taking care that
nothing is lost. His house and lands, whether rice-
fields, hills or woods are placed in your charge until
they can be sold later when the money must be paid
with the taxes to this Office. His two daughters are
already married and so are not affected by his punishment. Mind and pay attention to all this."

Of Sogoro's two daughters, who are here referred to
the oldest was named Ohatsu ; and had when nineteen married Yujiro, the son of Jiroemon, the headman
of Kinubashi in the Province of Hitachi in the dominions of Matsudaira Mutsu no Kami. She had one son.
Her younger sister was named Osen, and had been adopted by Gemba, who lived in the Province of Shimosa,
under the jurisdiction of Naito Geki. Her husband's
name was Tojuro. They had no connection with
Sogoro's history because they were under different
masters, but they were it is said warm friends and

loved each other very much. We cannot however go into particulars here, for fear of being too tedious.

CHAPTER XVI.

SOGORO AND HIS FAMILY ARE PUT TO DEATH.

Now Sogoro belonged to the temple of Toshoji. This temple is still to be seen in the village of Daikata, and at the time of our story, it was the most celebrated in the District—more so even than the temple of Butchoji in the village of Lower Iwahashi. On hearing of the intended execution, the Toshoji priests went to the authorities and begged them to spare the lives of Sogoro's wife and children ; but they were informed that it was impossible. They then asked permission to bury the bodies. The authorities replied : " Your Reverences can take the bodies of the four children, but the bodies of Sogoro and his wife will have to remain exposed for three days. If however you care to wait on the execution ground till the examining officers have all gone and then consult the men left on guard, you may perhaps succeed." This therefore they decided to do.

Now Kojima had resolved not to have any of the provincial officials to assist at the execution, and so had sent to the yashiki in Yedo, and summoned Ogawa and another inspector, together with a guard of twenty-four foot-soldiers. The day having arrived, Kojima went to the execution ground at Ebaradai, dressed in loose hunting trousers ; and with him Shinagawa and Ogawa and also the guard all armed with sticks.

As the report of the execution had spread far and wide, crowds of people of all ages, not only from the neighbouring villages but also from all the country side, flockèd together until even the large execution ground was filled to overflowing. Torn with grief at having to part from Sogoro, they pressed and crowded each other not a little in their attempts to secure good positions. Among them were the priests from Toshoji and twelve other temples with four coffins and two litters.

At the hour of the snake (10 a.m.) Sogoro and his wife were brought out bound to long poles. Their four children bound with ropes sat down on the rough straw. On seeing them, each one in the crowd whether old or young joined his hands and greeted Sogoro as a god, calling out : " Namu Sogoro Daimyojin " (i.e. Save us, oh Sogoro, thou great and famous god !) Not satisfied with this, they also threw rice-bread and cakes to the four children in such quantities that they fell like hail around them. These the foot-soldiers pushed away with their sticks, saying : " The children's hands are tied, so your presents can do them no good. You must not give them anything." The people however.threw them as fast as ever, saying : " That makes no difference, these are for them to take to the next world to enjoy there." Oh, it was indeed a sad sight !

Now when the appointed time had come, the eldest son Sohei was taken first to be put to death; and no one in the crowd cared to keep his eyes open to behold such a sight.   Ogawa stood forward and said :   " Your father Sogoro committed a grievous crime in presenting a petition to the Shogun ; and therefore you are condemned to be beheaded."   " Please wait a little," replied Sohei who was just thirteen.   " I am most thankful to you for so graciously allowing me to be executed for what my father Sogoro has done ; but I am afraid if I am beheaded in my parents' presence that it will cause them much grief, so I shall be called unfilial :   I therefore humbly implore you to punish me after they have been executed."   His head fell even before he had finished speaking.

The next son Gennosuke was then brought to the same spot.   He was ten years old and said :   " I have a boil on the right side of my neck, so please cut my head off from the left side."   Hardly had he said this when his head also fell.   The third son Kihachi who was just eight had barely time to utter a sound before his head also fell in the dust.

The Butchoji priest had been ill, and was still very weak but when he heard it was finally decided that the four children were to be executed, he hurried to the place of execution and reached there just as Rokunosuke, the fourth son, who was only four was brought out to die.   He at once took off his scarf and threw it towards the child but as he was so weak it did not reach Rokunosuke whose head fell at once. Shinagawa seeing what he had done, said :   " Why did not your Reverence come a little earlier ? " The priest could not reply for his tears.

It seemed like a dream, so terrible was it; and the continuous groans that went up from the crowd sounded almost as if a mountain were in eruption. Sogoro's wife Okin burst out into a wild laugh, and said : " Oh ! what noble children. Mind you don't forget what your father told you ! We are ready and willing to lay down our lives but can never forget how our four children have been so cruelly killed, murdered right before our eyes. How sorrowful ! How woeful ! " As she said this, she gnashed her teeth, her eyes glared, and her whole body trembled with rage.

Sogoro also laughed loudly, and said : " My wife ! How well you have spoken ! My life-long desire has been to lay down my life for all the people; but it is barbarous to slay our four children right before our very eyes. Our lord by his unjust rule was bringing trouble and death on all the people. He not only paid no attention to their sufferings ; but he refused our petitions, and thus compelled us to appeal direct to the Shogun. He is therefore the cause of this cruel execution and of all our misery ; and assuredly until our revenge is satisfied he shall have no peace." As he said this, he ground his teeth, and his tears of rage mingled with his blood.

As he finished, the executioners approached within sight of the wretched couple, brandishing their spears. Sogoro at once closed his eyes, and hardly had he done so, when he was speared on both sides so that the points projected above both his shoulders. Opening

his eyes again, he said to the lookers on : " I am
much obliged to you for so kindly praying for me.
Farewell now! Farewell! " As he said this, his wife
Okin was speared in the same way. Opening her eyes
just as her husband had done, she said : "Farewell
all of you." Without pausing to rest, the executioners
speared them again and again so that they said no
more. At this terrible sight, numbers of the spectators
fell down and rolled about on the grass crying out
and lamenting, so that the very ground shook.

Now as soon as Sogoro and his wife were dead, the
priests from Toshoji and the other temples went and
took the bodies of their four children ; and, amid
many lamentations, put them into the coffins they had
brought for the purpose. As they were putting in the
heads, the Butchoji priest seized Rokunosuke's, saying : " I will bury this one at my temple." The
Toshoji priest would not however agree to it, maintain-
ing that he had a right to bury them all as Sogoro and
his family had belonged to his temple. Then the
Butchoji priest said : " You can never save the lives
of any who have been condemned to death by asking
for them before they are brought to the place of execution like the common people do, for warriors are very
strict in carrying out their orders. If they once sentence anybody to death, they will never let him off.
But I hear that the inspector said that he would not
save the lives of these four children, even if asked to
do so. Why did he say that ? Was it not because
he hoped some one would ask him ? Having been
brought to the execution ground, they were as though

already executed. Why then did you not throw your scarf to them? And if that failed, you should have offered to die in their stead? Why did you stand there staring; and not try to save them? And now you say you have the right to bury them. You are far too greedy. You are ignorant of the first duties of a priest. When I threw my scarf, the inspector said it was too late, which certainly meant that he would have given me the child if I had come a little earlier. Had I saved him, I should have made him my disciple; and though I am grieved to say I was too late, I shall take possession of his head." So saying, he seized the head which had already been put into the coffin, and wrapping it in his dress went off.

At that, the Toshoji priest was furious and called out: "Go some one and bring him back." The people however had all been much influenced by what the Butchoji priest had said and were reluctant to move, so at last he went himself. The Butchoji priest seeing he was pursued, and feeling sure he should get the worst of it if he was caught, jumped into a large pool near by which forms part of the Imba Marsh, and died. One of the farmers, who had followed intending to help him if the worst came to the worst, saw him jump in; but was too far off to save him. Not wishing the Toshoji priest to gain possession of the head, he stood on the bank when the priest came up and called out: "Neither the priest's body nor the child's head are here." This he repeated so often that at last the priest went off, saying he could find neither the body nor the head. Thus they were both left to

THE FUNERAL.

Page 16.

fertilize the weeds that grew in the marsh ; and to this
day, the farmers in that neighbourhood never speak of
it without tears.

Now when the inspector and the officials belonging
to the guard had all withdrawn, one of the watch said :
" It is nearly dark and we are all going home now.
Take down the other two bodies, if you care to, and
bury them carefully, but you must leave the posts just
as they are." In a short time, all the soldiers had
gone and there were only the headmen and the priests
left. Two young men at once climbed the poles and
soon jumped down each with one of the bodies in his
arms. It was then seen that they were Sogoro's two
sons-in-law. As they touched the ground their wives
rushed forward and embraced the bodies so closely
that the villagers could hardly distinguish the living
from the dead. Then they rolled about crying and
lamenting. The people however hastened to stop them,
saying : " Remember we are stealing the bodies
secretly, you must not make such a noise." By alter-
nate threats and persuasions, they at last succeeded in
quieting them and put both the bodies in the litters.
The women were so worn out with grief that they
would not have been able to walk even to the temple,
had not their husbands taken their hands and support-
ed them along. The bodies were buried in the presence of all the farmers of the district who flocked in
crowds to the funeral.

Now Zembei, Heijuro and Hanyemon, Sogoro's
trusty friends, retired after witnessing his execution to
Zenkoji in Shinshiu, and after staying there a short

time went on to Koyasan. A few months later, Heijuro was taken ill and died at the early age of forty-
seven, heartbroken at having had to separate from
Sogoro.

Hanyemon, who had shaved his head and become a
priest, being now called Yushin, went shortly after to
Shinagawa in the neighbourhood of Yedo, and there
erected a stone image in honour of the god Jizo. He
lived there for many years, spending his days and
nights in praying for the happiness of Sogoro and his
family. He died in 1671, having attained the age of
threescore and ten.

As for Zembei, he, known now as the priest Zensho,
had the good fortune to return to his native place;
and there he lived, thinking constantly of Sogoro and
his family, and praying continually for their salvation.
He passed away in the 10th month of the 2nd year of
Empo (Nov. 1674.) Long years afterwards, the names
of these three faithful men were remembered and held
in high esteem.

CHAPTER XVII.

KOZUKE NO SUKE RECEIVES THE REPORT OF SOGORO'S EXECUTION.

Now Kojima and Shinagawa, together with the
twenty-four foot-soldiers, returned as they had been
ordered, direct to Yedo from the execution ground;

while Asai and Takamachi waited till the next morning, when they set out early and arrived safely at the yashiki in Yedo the same night. Immediately on arriving, Kojima presented himself before his master Kozuke no Suke, who however cruel he might be, yet could not feel comfortable, thinking of the barbarous death of Sogoro and his family. He had put on his official dress ; and when Kojima went in, was sitting erect on the mats. When Kojima had finished giving him the chief particulars of the execution, Kozuke no Suke said : " It was about the hour of the snake (10 a.m.) when they were executed, wasn't it ? " Kojima replied : " Yes, a little past." Hearing that, Kozuke no Suke bowed his head in sorrow and was silent for a little while. He then said : " Tell me, did not Sogoro curse me, and say that he should revenge himself on me for all his sufferings ? " Kojima answered : " No : he did not. He and his wife were very quiet and seemed well prepared. They simply asked the spectators to pray for their future happiness and then, after saying a few words to us they died." Kozuke no Suke again said : " A little after 10 o'clock, my eyes were suddenly blinded, and I seemed to hear a crowd crying out with sorrow. I could not make it out, and so thought it must be caused by Sogoro and his wife cursing and reproaching me ; but if it was as you say, I can rest easy." As he spoke, he looked quite scared. Kojima was greatly astonished and could only bow and retire feeling sure that his master's terror was the result of Sogoro's curse. Just then it struck 7 p.m. and Kozuke no Suke lay down just as he was, without

even calling for a pillow; but no sooner did he begin
to doze than he heard the cries of Sogoro's ghost and
started up at once, saying: "How curious! How
strange!" Calling some of his courtiers, he asked
them whether they had heard the cries; but they
assured him that they had heard nothing. This made
him still more confused, and whether he would or no
Sogoro's death was constantly present to his mind.

The next morning, he sent for Shinagawa and asked
him for full particulars about the execution. Shinagawa
was naturally straightforward and so would not use
flattery, moreover though not a philanthropist he utterly detested all cruelty. Being a man of such a disposition, he had been much pained by the barbarous
punishment of Sogoro; and on hearing his master's request thought to himself: "How fortunate it is that he
has asked me," and replied: "Sogoro was a man of
greater courage than I had thought. He must have possessed some ability too; for he managed to save all the
farmers in a district yielding 40,000 koku annually and
relieved all their troubles when their struggle seemed
quite hopeless. Knowing how much they owe him,
many thousands of them were present at his execution and each one joined his hands and shouted through
his tears: 'Namu Sogoro Daimyojin! Namu Sogoro
Daimyojin!' (i.e. Save us, oh Sogoro, thou great and
famous god!) Thus you see they really worshipped
him as a god even while he was yet alive.
His wife was so excited by seeing her four children
executed right before her very eyes that she looked
almost like a devil as with bloodshot eyes she screamed

out: 'How barbarous an execution is this! However great their father's crime was, it is barbarous to
kill such young children right in front of their parents'
eyes. Living or dying, we shall certainly avenge
their deaths.' As I listened, my hair stood on end
with fear." Hearing this, Kozuke no Suke felt
half repentant; but was vexed at himself for being
so and therefore vented all his wrath on Shinagawa,
saying : " It is only cowardly fellows like you whose
hair would stand on end at that. Sogoro must have
been a thoroughly bad man thus to have forgotten his
own great crime and cherished revenge towards his
superiors! How can he possibly injure me? The
story you have just told me cannot be true, it is so
very different from the account Kojima gave me. You
must have made it up." Hearing this, Shinagawa
forgot himself, and retorted : " All my life I never
once told a lie and even if I told one now, what good
would it do as there are thousands of spectators who
were there and know all that took place. You had
better ask some of them. It is said to be useless
to remonstrate about a thing that is already past ;
but I wish to say a few words, hoping they may
be useful in the future. In heaven and earth there
is no affection so strong as that which exists between a parent and his child. Even the birds and
beasts love their offspring, much more man. It was
very cruel of you to behead Sogoro's four children
right before his eyes ; and so he and his wife revenged
themselves by cursing and reviling you. By so
doing, they in the first place alienated the hearts

of your subjects from you ; in the second place, they
disgraced your country and injured your reputation,
and thus will bring misfortune on you and prevent
your descendants flourishing. I therefore beseech
you strictly to examine the provincial officials
who oppressed the people and thus caused them so
much suffering. Please be very strict with them. It
was only natural that the farmers should call Sogoro a
god ; and the best way to satisfy them, is for you to
establish a temple and enshrine him there as a god.
If you do this, you will turn away his curse. You
ought also to alter your behaviour and treat your subjects more mercifully. Your house will then become
more and more flourishing, and surely no reward can
exceed this. Please consider this matter carefully."

Kozuke no Suke was very angry at hearing Shinagawa's remonstrances, and said : "What a terrible
chatterbox you are! Who said that Sogoro was a
god? Was it not his followers and those who had
been greatly benefitted by his presenting their petition
to the Shogun ; and who, seeing him on the point of
being executed, naturally felt bound to flatter him.
You are an insolent fellow to dare to presume to
teach me, your master, how to examine my subjects."
He thus scolded him wildly, but Shinagawa replied :
"Please tell me where my fault lies." Kozuke no
Suke said : "You did wrong in that though you were
sent to the execution as an inspector, you failed to
make any report to me on your return. What is the
use of such service?" Hearing this, Shinagawa straight-
ening himself up, said : "I thought of coming to you

last night directly I came in ; but, as it was about half
past nine Mr. Kojima told me that as it was so late
you would probably have retired to rest and so there
would be no objection to my waiting till this morning.
He also promised to mention my return to some of the
courtiers so that you might hear of it. As such was
his wish, I had no choice but to put off seeing you till
this morning when I received your summons and so
came at once."   Still more annoyed at receiving such
a reply, Kozuke no Suke said :   " You talkative fellow !   From this time I cannot allow you to come into
my presence.   Go home and stay there in confinement."   As there was no help for it, Shinagawa retired
crestfallen, lamenting the danger that seemed to threaten his lord's house.   The other courtiers tried repeatedly to have him excused, but in vain ; and at last
Kozuke no Suke banished him to Sakura.

As soon as Kozuke no Suke realized how Kojima
had deceived him he said such a cowardly soldier was
no use to him and obliged him to retire into seclusion.
Kojima was not however a bad man.   He only spoke
as he did, thinking if he told his master plainly how
angry Sogoro and his wife were, it would trouble him
and thus only hasten the misfortune with which they
had threatened him ; but he made a mistake in not
arranging it first with Shinagawa : perhaps however, it
could not even then have been prevented ; for it is said
that when a country is about to perish, a remarkable
calamity always happens first, and so it was in this case.

After Kojima's dismissal, the other officials met together at the Yedo Office and spent many hours in

consultation. They were unanimous in feeling that the reason for such a disturbance rising then must lie in the avarice and oppression of the provincial officials ; and felt it essential that they should all be carefully examined and properly punished. But as Kojima had just been ordered to resign, and Shinagawa had been banished to Sakura, both of them having incurred their master's displeasure simply by disagreeing in the verbal accounts they had given him of the execution, the other officials hesitated to go and ask him to examine the provincial officials knowing well what a cruel and quick-tempered man he was. At last however one of them, named Tanabe, volunteered to go. Entering his lord's presence, he said : " We believe that Sogoro's crime was after all the result of the avarice and oppression of the provincial officials ; and we have therefore been expecting you to order them to be examined, but as yet we have heard nothing. I therefore ventured to come and ask what you intend doing about it." " Why," replied Kozuke no Suke, " that is your business, it is silly of you to wait for my orders. Do as you like about it." " What you say," continued Tanabe, " is most reasonable. It is however very difficult for an official to examine any of his colleagues without having received an order from his master." Kozuke no Suke said : " As the petition from the farmers has been granted, and Sogoro has been punished there is nothing else to be done, so let it remain as it is." As there was no help for it, Tanabe withdrew. On hearing what had taken place, the other officials were thunderstruck, and said : " The lord of a castle ought not to act like this. If he only punishes the farmers and pays no attention to the behaviour of his servants, criminals will all the time become more and more numerous." They consulted together for some time but with no result as not one of them was willing to take the risk and boldly remonstrate with his lord.

CHAPTER XVIII.

KANAZAWA AND IKEURA BOTH COMMIT SUICIDE.

A few days after the events recorded in the last chapter, my lord Kozuke no Suke went to the palace and told how he had punished Sogoro. When the Shogun Iemitsu heard about it, he called Kawachi no Kami, one of his lords, and said: "Kawachi, was that a suitable punishment?" Now, though my lord Kawachi no Kami had read the petition, he did not like, wise though he was, to answer such a question, so he bowed low but said nothing. Seeing his confusion, the Shogun said: " Never mind. Never mind." So the matter ended.

After leaving the Shogun's presence, my lord Kawachi no Kami consulted with my lord Kuse Yamato no Kami who had also read the petition. These two lords lamented Kozuke no Suke's neglect in omitting to bring to trial his own servants who had by their cruelty driven Sogoro to slight the procession of the Shogun and thus lose his life, and they both felt that it was most unjust to leave it as it was.

The next day therefore when Kozuke no Suke went to the palace, one of them went up to him and said: "Sogoro, one of the farmers in your dominions certainly committed a grievous crime recently in forcing his petition on the Shogun, but at the same time it is well known that all such petitions have their origin in oppressive government. I do not think you are to blame, but you ought most certainly to examine your servants and see whether the fault does not lie with some of them. It is not really my business as through the merits of your ancestors the District has come to you; but in one sense at least the people are Imperial subjects, so I shall be much pleased to hear what you intend doing."

Kozuke no Suke was greatly perplexed, but remembering Tanabe's advice to him only the day before, he said: "It is a great disgrace to me and I hardly know what to do, but there must as you say be some among my servants who are to blame. A few days since therefore I sent two or three whom I could thoroughly rely on to look into the matter and will let you know the result."

"Why do you not go and examine into it yourself," continued the other? "If you do as you have just proposed, I am afraid that it will never be settled. If you need any help I shall be glad to assist you, so please feel quite free to ask me."

Blushing with vexation, Kozuke no Suke went home and at once sent for Tanabe and said : " I have thought carefully over what you said the other day about examining the provincial officials and am convinced that it will not do to leave them as they are after having executed Sogoro. They must be examined strictly and those who have done wrong must be brought here and punished. This cannot be accomplished unless a large number of officers are sent, so select those you think most suitable."

Hearing this, Tanabe went out and conferred for some time with his colleagues as to who should go but as none of them would undertake the task he at last called Takamachi, and said : " You must go for one, and Ogawa, and Hara, and I will go with you."

" When the farmers came before and were sent to the lower yashiki," replied Takamachi, " I asked that the matter might be investigated, but this was refused and so all this trouble has arisen. Now therefore, I would much rather be excused. If however you really wish me to go I must have full authority to punish the guilty ones and even have them put to death without having to consult with any one else. It is not such a difficult job and if you do this I shall need no one but Ogawa."

Knowing his ability, all the other officials were greatly delighted at his offer, and my lord Kozuke no Suke was much relieved, and summoning Takamachi gave him a dagger, saying : " You have full authority to act just as you think best, but there is one thing I want you to remember. When I was at court yesterday, my colleagues strongly advised me to examine into this matter. I wish you therefore to make a large number of criminals apparently but to have very few in reality."

Takamachi withdrew saying: "Your orders shall have my attention." The next morning he started before sunrise with Ogawa. On reaching Sakura, they summoned all the officials and spoke to them, saying: "Sogoro was crucified a little while since for having committed an atrocious crime but the reason for his crime must after all be sought in the misconduct of some of you officials. Our lord has therefore ordered us to investigate the matter strictly and punish the guilty ones. But first of all, why is Mr. Ikeura not here to-day, he is the governor of this District and so must know all about such a disturbance as this?"

Kanazaki replied: "As you no doubt remember he was ill when you were over last November and he has not been at the Office since."

Takamachi then turned to Kanazawa saying: "Everything connected with the farmers is under your direction as superintendent; and yet, when by your oppression you led them to present a petition, you re-fused to receive it, and so not only drove them to take it to Yedo where they made a great disturbance, but also impelled them to present it to his Lordship Kuse Yamato no Kami as he was going to the court and finally to force it on the Shogun. For so doing, Sogoro, his wife and four children have lost their lives; but as all this was really your doing as super-intendent, it is impossible for you to escape unpunished.

You must go to the Yedo Office and if you have anything to say, say it there." Speechless with horror, Kanazawa could make no reply.

The other officials were then examined so strictly that they were all much terrified and could only tremble and remain silent. Takamachi then sent a messenger to Ikeura, saying : " I have come here by our lord's orders to examine every one in the Office, so you must come there at once. If you are unable to walk, you can be carried."

Ikeura made answer, saying : " What nonsense to talk of examining me ! Even supposing you have come here by our lord's orders which I greatly doubt, there is no reason why you should presume to examine me. It is absurd to send a messenger to me while I am ill. If you wish to see me, you must come to my house."

On receiving this reply, Takamachi immediately sent saying : " Do you dare to disobey our lord's orders simply because my rank is low ? This is public business and I cannot come to your house ; but I assure you that if I go back to Yedo and tell our master how you have treated me, he will certainly summon you at once and then your regrets will all be in vain."

Ikeura replied : " I cannot understand why a madman like Takamachi has been sent from Yedo while Mr. Kojima is there so I have written a letter asking how it is and order you to take it to Yedo at once."

Hearing that, Takamachi became extremely angry and said : " You cowardly samurai ! You pretend to be ill every time I come ! It is not surprising that calamities should happen frequently to a country governed by such a baby. If I go back to Yedo like this, you must look out for the consequences ! "

With these words, he left Sakura at once and went back to Yedo full of shame that his attempts at examination had failed so utterly and vexed at the injury thereby done to his reputation. On hearing his report, my lord Kozuke no Suke was extremely angry and lost no time in dispatching a messenger to Sakura ordering Ikeura to go to Yedo instantly.

Now, as soon as Takamachi had left for Yedo, Ikeura sent for Kanazawa secretly, and said : " I sent Takamachi back as I did not care to be examined by a two year old baby like him. I expect however to be summoned to Yedo in a few days ; and so, as there is no way for me to escape, I would commit suicide now if it were not that everybody would then say that I had done it because I could not clear myself and that is just what I do not want. I intend going to our lord's presence as soon as he sends for me and shall there kill myself honourably. As for you, if you are brought to trial, you will certainly be ordered to commit harakiri, so you had better make up your mind and kill yourself at once, only do not do it until you hear from me again."

On receiving the summons to go to Yedo, Ikeura at once informed Kanazawa, and added : " As I told you the other day, I know that it is impossible for me to escape with my life, so now is the time for you to kill yourself and I will commit harakiri at the yashiki in Yedo." Kanazawa hearing that, turned pale and trembled all over. As he went back to his house, he thought to himself: "When Mitsuhashi ran away, Ikeura and I got off scot free by laying all the blame on him. That was all Ikeura's plot and I am quite sure that his object now in wishing me to kill myself is that he may save his own skin by laying all the blame on me. I do not half like it." He racked his brains to try and find some way of defeating Ikeura's plans ; but being naturally very dull and cowardly, he could think of nothing at this crisis in his life ; so calling his servant Kiroku, he told him all about the matter and then added : "I know when I am dead the governor means to save himself by laying all the blame of his own crimes on me but this is more than I can put up with. The proverb says : 'When you are in a fix, consult some one even if it be only your own knees.' I wish therefore to consult you about it."

Kiroku replied : "Indeed sir, the governor doubt-less intends in the bottom of his heart doing as you say ; but after all you have come to a point where you cannot escape, and if you try to do so you will only be laughed at as childish. You had better therefore give me a memorandum with full particulars of everything in regard to the compulsory service and the increased annual taxation : for it is said that a dying bird sings sadly and a dying man speaks the truth. Now that you are so near the end of your life why should you quarrel with the governor? If however he tries to save himself by laying the blame of all his crimes on you, I will send your note to the Yedo Office ; but if he kills himself honourably, I shall not send it, so whatever happens you can rest assured that all will be right. You can therefore die without anxiety."

Kanazawa was much perplexed at hearing that there was no way for him to escape but took pen and paper, and though all of a tremble managed to write a memorandum which he gave to Kiroku. Then going into an inner room, he there put an end to himself by committing harakiri.

After hearing of his death, Ikeura set out without further delay for Yedo. On reaching the yashiki there, he tried to shield himself by pretending that he had been ill most of the time, and was too old and feeble to go often to the Office. He stated that he had not known anything of the way the farmers were being oppressed until after Kanazawa's death when he at once saw how it was. All that he acknowledged was his neglect in not having looked into the matter before.

Kozuke no Suke said : "In this petition the farmers state that they presented it to you first. Why then did you not receive it and examine into their grievances ? "

Ikeura replied : "As you say, they did come to me first but I was ill in bed at the time ; and when I heard the noise, I sent one of my servants out to see what was the matter. He came back saying that the farmers had come with a petition, so I told him to tell them to go to Kanazawa, and they went away at once. This is all I know about it."

Kozuke no Suke put several other questions to him, to all of which he replied without in any way incriminating himself. As there was nothing else to be done, he was confined in the barracks and there examined

by Asai and Takamachi, but they both failed to bring
home any crime to him : so at last they sent for the
headmen from two or three of the villages in the
dominion, and asked them to state what happened
when they first presented their petition.

One of them named Ichinojo said : " We went first
of all to the Office and presented our petition there.
It was received at first but in a few minutes was
returned. We then went in a body to the gate of the
governor's house and presented it there. Mr. Kagawa
came out and took it in to the governor but soon
brought it back again, saying : ' The governor is very
cruel. He will not receive your petition. I cannot
serve such a hard master.' He then absconded at once."

Asai and Takamachi examined Ikeura in connection with this statement, but he replied : " That
man Kagawa was one of my attendants. I sent him
to take the farmers to Kanazawa but he was carried
away by his avarice and so accepted bribes from them
promising to help them. I scolded him for this and
for not taking them to Kanazawa, and as he could not
clear himself, he ran away saying what a cruel master
I was. What an audacious man Ichinojo is to try and
deceive you so! Bring him here, and I will soon show
you he is wrong."

When the headmen went into Ikeura's presence he
glared at them fiercely, and said : " You bribed
Kagawa and so enabled him to run away ; and now, not
knowing where he is, you have the audacity to try and
lay the blame of not receiving your petition on me ; but
as you made him run away, you must find him and

bring him here without delay, otherwise I shall lose
my reputation."

Quite appalled at his rage, Ichinojo was unable to
say a single word in reply but turned to Takamachi
and said : " Please allow us to withdraw. We shall
want some time for consideration before we can give
any more evidence." They were therefore sent back
to the ostler's again.

Now it so happened that Kanazawa's old servant
Kiroku, having lost his place on his master's death,
had come in his wanderings to Yedo and was staying
at the same ostler's as a sort of hanger on, at the same
time keeping his eye on Ikeura.

He overheard the headmen consulting together and
said : " Am I right in supposing that Mr. Ikeura is
now trying to shield himself by laying all the blame of
his own crimes on Mr. Kanazawa, my late master ? He
knew he could not escape and so put an end to himself
recently by committing harakiri. I have a note here
which he wrote just before he died and which I feel
sure will help you."

The headmen were greatly delighted and taking
Kiroku with them went at once to the yashiki. Takamachi and Asai were much pleased to see them and
at once summoning Ikeura, they read the note aloud
as follows :—

To Messrs. Takamachi and Ogawa,
        Officers at the Yedo Office.
    When you were here recently, you said
    that I was to blame for all the trouble which
    had been caused by the petition which the

farmers of this District presented last year. If however you will be so kind as to read this note, you will see that I was not acting on my own responsibility at all, but was ordered by Mr. Ikeura to do as I did.

In regard to the money paid as thank-offerings; an insurrection had broken out in Amakusa, and I was told that money must be collected for war preparations as it might be wanted in a hurry at almost any time. Not knowing what to do, I asked Mr. Ikeura; and he told me that it was to be collected in the form of thank-offerings from those who married, built houses, or adopted sons; so I went all round the villages in the District collecting it. The insurrection in Amakusa was soon put down; but, as universal peace did not reign throughout the country, it was determined to continue levying the taxes, pretending that they were to provide cavalry and to furnish the retainers with the necessaries of war.

As to the taxes on horses; Denzo, who had been in Mr. Ikeura's employ before, came one day and asked to be appointed horse-inspector. He stated that horse stealing was very common; and promised, if appointed, to do his utmost to find any horses that might be stolen from any of the farmers in the District and return them to their rightful owners. Mr. Ikeura therefore appointed him and ordered me to arrange for him to have a daily ration to be provided for by a tax on every horse that was bought or exchanged. He also directed me to prepare a register for him ; so I made one and wrote on its cover, ' Register of Cattle and Horses.' I do not however know anything about the money which was collected as Mr. Ikeura arranged about that himself. When however Matsusuke was arrested, Denzo's true character was discovered and he was banished at the request of the headmen of the District ; but the tax having been levied by Mr. Ikeura's orders, was collected as before.

As to the increase in the annual tax ; the governor told me our lord had ordered him to levy a certain amount of rice annually when the harvest was good and store it up ready to help the people when their crops were bad. When I asked him how much increase I should make, he replied 25%. I therefore made a register putting down an increase of one to and two sho to the koku or about 24%.

In addition to the above ; I levied other duties and exacted compulsory service in accordance with Mr. Ikeura's orders.

I suspected several times that it was unjust to extort from the farmers the taxes mentioned above ; but as the governor had ordered me to do so, I could not well refuse. I now confess

that I did wrong in thus yielding. I beseech
you however to remember that I never en-
riched myself by them in any way whatever.

Kanazawa Joemon.

As Takamachi finished, Ikeura seeing the note was
not in Kanazawa's own writing burst out laughing, and
said: "That is a very suspicious looking letter, let
me look at it." Takamachi without the least hesitation held it out to him upside down. Ikeura stretched
out his hand and seized it, saying: "My old eyes
can not read it so far off." He then without waiting
a moment tore it all to pieces leaving only the part
which bore the signature and put the pieces into the
fire, saying: "You are extremely audacious to try to
convict me with a forgery like that. I have, as you
see, carefully kept the part on which the signature was
written. There are sure to be some letters in the
house from Kanazawa. Go and bring one and compare
it with this. It will be a bad job for you if this is not
his signature." "Fortunately," said Asai, "I have a
note in my pocket-book which I received from him the
other day." He took it out and was horrified to see
that the signature on the scrap was not Kanazawa's
writing at all. Takamachi however did not seem at
all disturbed, but said: "Ikeura! you ought not to
boast so. You have behaved most insolently in thus
destroying an important letter. If you persist in
alleging that it was forged, you will have an opportunity of proving it in the court. The one you have
just destroyed was only a copy. The original is here."

So saying, he took out another letter and showed it but was very careful not to let go of it. Then rolling it up again, he put it back in his bosom, saying : "We are both examining you by our master's orders, but as you are so rude to us we will just go and tell him how you are behaving." So saying, they both left him and told Kozuke no Suke all that had taken place. When he had heard it, he was extremely angry and at once summoned Ikeura and all the other officials. As soon as they presented themselves, Kozuke no Suke handed Takamachi a written order which he ordered him to read at once. He accordingly read as follows :—

> As it was reported that you Ikeura had been guilty of many improper acts, you were placed in confinement. You have however shown much obstinacy and self-will during your examination and have not acted at all as became your station. You are therefore deprived of your rank and ordered to take the · lowest seat. You are warned too that you must act with more respect during the remainder of your trial.

Ikeura was much astonished at this and turned pale. Takamachi rising, bowed politely to all the other officials and asked them to excuse him as he was only doing his duty. He then said to Ikeura : "You can not disobey your lord's orders. Do as you were ordered and take the lowest seat." Ikeura, proud as he was, rose slowly and reluctantly took the bottom seat. Takamachi then took out Kanazawa's real letter and laying it down in front of Ikeura, said: "How now? Do you recognize this as Kanazawa's writing, or do you persist in asserting that it is a forgery?" On seeing it, Ikeura was dumb. At last he replied: "It would be very easy for me to clear myself but Kanazawa is dead, and so it is no good now to go into the rights and wrongs of the case: besides if I did, I should leave a bad name behind me. I will therefore say nothing." "Then," said Asai, "the trial is over. The sentence will be pronounced after we know our master's will in the matter. You can go." Ikeura went to his house guarded by Nomura, and that night he thought over the crimes he had committed, and saw that he had brought his punishment on himself and that all regrets were useless. He thought the best way was to put an end to his own life and so escape being laughed at afterwards for having allowed himself to be executed by his lord. Luckily for him, the men on guard were fast asleep; and so, as there was no one to hinder him, he killed himself. The following was found the next day fastened to one of the wooden doors in front of his house: "A snake named Kanazawa that was in Ikeura's bosom died, but his bones were not picked up." It sometimes happens that three or four who call themselves bosom friends unite together to annoy their neighbours and defy their masters, but they cannot succeed in the end once in ten thousand times. Even those who have been looked upon as the closest friends will, when desperate, become as snakes or frogs hurting and devouring one another. This ought to warn us to be careful.

CHAPTER XIX.

THE GHOSTS BEGIN TORMENTING KOZUKE NO SUKE AFTER FIRST KILLING HIS WIFE.

After Ikeura's death, Asai, Takamachi and Hara went to Sakura and examined the officials there, banishing thirteen and sentencing thirty-nine to other punishments—some were imprisoned, others were confined to their own houses, while others again were simply degraded. It was said however in the report to the Shogun that eight had been ordered to commit harakiri.

When Kozuke no Suke went with this report to the court, he was told that an order had been issued requiring him to examine minutely into the decrease in the population of all the 136 villages in his dominions. If it was found that any people had been driven by poverty to remove, they were to be sought out and made to return; and were to receive five dollars each for repairing their houses, and to be given a plough and all other necessary implements free of charge. He was also informed that if any were not found, he would be held responsible. Certainly this was a most benevolent order for the farmers.

Now, towards the end of November, my lord Kozuke no Suke's wife who was just twenty-one was suddenly seized with violent pains; and grew rapidly worse, till by the beginning of December, she was suffering

KOZUKE NO SUKE AND THE GHOSTS.

... Saka no Suke was in great ... and ... in many ... his ... grew steadily worse. Also ... lights began to be seen ... about her bedroom and sometimes she heard screams and mocking laughter. These terrified her and greatly increased her sufferings so that her whole body was ... to ... and she often had fearful convulsions. Seeing her torments, one of the priests in attendance went to Hara and told him about it. He was much surprised and seizing his sword rushed to the ... court where he was met by my lord Kuroda no Suke who taking him into the next room, said: " My wife says that there are lights flying about her room, and sometimes she also hears screams; but I can neither see the lights nor hear the voices. Go and look whether you can see anything." Hara ... ... and going to the room, at once saw ... flying about the bed; he also heard faint ... He came ... to the conclusion that the ... lights were the ... of ... and his wife, but he ... ... what to do. One of the ... ... the ... from the fire and looked about like a maniac; as with sash untied, dress flying, and hair in confusion 'she rushed about the room vainly endeavouring to catch the lights. Some of the other women were also running about trying to help her to the ... After watching them a little while, Hara ... ... of the other lights, saying: " You ... ... the spirits of Yogoro and his wife. I know ... ... here but I ask you to go away and ... ... I am Hara."

severely. Kozuke no Suke was in great trouble and called in many famous physicians, but his wife grew steadily worse. Also, wonderful to relate, lights began to be seen moving about her bedroom and sometimes she heard screams and mocking laughter. These terrified her and greatly increased her sufferings so that her whole body was bathed in hot sweat and she often had fearful convulsions. Seeing her torments, one of the priests in attendance went to Hara and told him about it. He was much surprised and seizing his sword rushed to the inner court where he was met by my lord Kozuke no Suke who taking him into the next room, said : " My wife says that there are lights flying about her room, and sometimes she also hears screams ; but I can neither see the lights nor hear the voices. Go and look whether you can see anything." Hara cheerfully obeyed ; and going to the room, at once saw two lights flying about the bed : he also heard faint screams. He soon came to the conclusion that the two lights were the souls of Sogoro and his wife, but for a little while was puzzled what to do. One of the nurses had seized the tongs from the fire and looked almost like a maniac, as with sash untied, dress flying, and hair in confusion she rushed about the room vainly endeavouring to catch the lights. Some of the other women were also running about trying to help her in the chase. After watching them a little while, Hara went into the room and spoke to the lights, saying : " You must surely be the spirits of Sogoro and his wife. I know well why you have come here but I ask you to go away just for to-night. I am Hara."

Wonderful to relate, the lights disappeared at once and the cries and laughs were heard no more that night. This must have been because Hara had treated the people so kindly when he lived at Sakura : indeed, when he moved to Yedo, they were so sorry to lose him that a great many of them went with him as far as Funabashi.

As Hara was so successful the first night in driving the ghosts away, my lord Kozuke no Suke ordered him to keep watch in the sick-room every night. By degrees however, the ghosts became more and more troublesome and refused to go away even at his request. Seeing this, my lord Kozuke no Suke said to him one day : "How is it you were able to drive away the ghosts the first time you tried ? " He replied : " My lord, are you not convinced yet that they are the avenging spirits of Sogoro and his wife whom you put to death so cruelly last spring ? At first they listened to my request and went away, but of late they pay no attention at all to me. I am very tired and should be so glad if you could let some one else take my place to-night." Kozuke no Suke said : " All right. You are quite wrong in thinking they are the spirits of Sogoro and his wife, and it is quite useless for you to watch with that notion in your head. Go at once and rest." Hara thanked him and withdrew, too tired by far to notice his master's displeasure.

Now Kawamura's son Kaheiji, whom we mentioned in a previous chapter, was one of Kozuke no Suke's attendants ; but was such a coward that he used to break out into a cold perspiration all over whenever

he heard the others only talking about the ghosts.
Imagine then his terror when he was ordered to
keep watch in the room where the ghosts actually
appeared. He racked his brains for some way to get
out of it, but not finding any, and not daring to disobey
his master's orders, he went trembling to the room.
That night the ghosts of both Sogoro and his wife appeared transfixed with spears, and looking just as they
did when they were being crucified. Going close to
the sick lady's pillow, they stood there crying : " Woe !
Woe ! " It was a fearful sight. Kaheiji groaned with
fright, and at last fell fainting to the floor. The other
attendants also lost their heads and rushed about,
calling out : " There ! look there ! " While they were
doing so, the ghosts seized the sick lady and turning
her over, beat her till the sad end came. They both
then vanished instantly. When it was known that she
was really dead, the excitement in the house increased
and spread to the retainers whose agitation and sorrow
knew no bounds. Kozuke no Suke went at once to
his wife's room, and in the extremity of his grief took
hold of her corpse, saying : " It is sad to think of how
all through your illness, you were tormented by evil
spirits and died such an unmerited death." Then
jumping up suddenly and seizing his sword, he cried
out : " You evil spirits, you shall not escape ! " With
these words, he struck at a maid who was standing
near, cutting her right in two. Striking a second
blow, he wounded Kuwayama so severely that he
had barely strength to crawl away. All this time,
Kaheiji had been lying on the floor but in the excite-

ment some one now trod on him. Up he jumped at
once, crying out : " What terrible spirits these are !
Come all of you and let us fight them ! " Kozuke no
Suke said : " Is that Kaheiji ? Do not let them
escape." Encouraged by his master's words, he who
had been such a coward before, drew his sword and
rushed about brandishing it.

Now Hara, hearing how Kozuke no Suke's wife
had died and how his master had killed one of his
servants and wounded another, seized his sword and
hastened to the palace. Reaching there he crept
into the room and caught Kozuke no Suke from
behind. He turned round and said : " Hara, you
are too late. I have just seen the ghosts, and am
convinced that they are as you said Sogoro and his
wife, though I never saw them while they were
alive. Sogoro has escaped but I have disabled his
wife and am now looking for him with Kaheiji."
He spoke very clearly and did not show the least
sign of madness. A candle was lighted and the
room examined, but nothing could be found except
the bleeding body of the maid lying on the floor. On
seeing it, Hara asked in surprise what had happened.
Kozuke no Suke said : " I thought she was Sogoro's
wife. What a pity that I was so stupid ! But who did
I take for Sogoro ? I felt my sword bite when I hit at
him, so he must be wounded too." His remorse was
terrible. As the disturbance in the bedroom gradually
calmed down, the maidens and the officials who had all
run away went back, and were very glad to see that
their master had recovered his senses. A great crowd

followed him to the outer court. The funeral passed
off quietly and for more than ten days after there was
no sign of the spirits.

In the following year, that is to say, in the 3rd. year of
Shoho, on the night of the 6th. of the 1st. Month (Feb.
12th. 1646), a loud voice was heard in the large room
of the palace, calling out: " Woe! Woe! Cursed!
Cursed! " The officers on watch lighted their lanterns
and searched all over; but when they looked in one
room, they heard the ghosts in another; and when they
looked there, sounds of laughter came from the room
they had just left. They looked in the drawing-room,
the messengers' room, the large central room ; and in
all the other rooms, prying into all the corners, but
could see nothing, so at last they gave up the search
in despair.

About twelve o'clock the same night, the spirits
again appeared and stood by Kozuke no Suke's pillow.
He drew his sword and brandished it when they
disappeared at once. This would go on ten or fifteen
nights in succession and then nothing would be seen for
two or three weeks, when the spirits would come out
again ; and so it went on for about four years till my lord
Kozuke no Suke could hardly sleep at all and looked
very sadly. Seeing this, Hara went to him and said:
" For four years the spirits of Sogoro and his wife have
been tormenting you by appearing at frequent intervals.
Though you are not ill, you look most wretched, and
your servants are all very much afraid that some great
calamity will befall your house. They have therefore
sent me to ask you to make Sogoro a god and allow

the farmers in your dominions to worship him. By so
doing, you will please the spirits and thus lessen their
hatred, and your house will then enjoy security and
peace. If you will allow me to do so, I will send word
to the provincial officials to establish a temple at once."
" Don't bother yourselves about me ! " replied Kozuke
no Suke, " I am not troubled like my poor wife used
to be. The ghosts certainly do come sometimes;
but they are such cowards they always go away
directly I draw my sword. Many people have been
deified for some virtue that they possessed ; but what
virtue can any one find in Sogoro, and who would
care to worship such a good for nothing fellow even
if he were deified? Let him be and don't trouble
yourself about him ! " In fine, so decided did he
seem, that Hara had nothing for it but to return to
the Office and tell how he had fared. All the officials
were very sorry indeed but did not know what to do
next, so the days passed in worry and anxiety.

About three years later, on the 11th. of the 2nd.
month in the 2nd. year of Keian (March 13th 1649)
loud shouts, like the war-cry of twenty or thirty
thousand troops rushing on the town, were suddenly
heard in Sakura in the middle of the day. The castle
shook fearfully and the people rushed out of their
houses in terror and were horrified to see a man and
woman hanging in the air just above the town. They
seemed to be transfixed with spears, and all the people
could hear their cries : " How woeful ! How sorrowful ! Before this year is over, we shall have taken
the revenge we decided on long since and which has

but increased as the months and years passed by."
They then vanished; and as they did so, it sounded
as if all the roofs and ceilings in the place were falling.   As was only natural, the people were very
much frightened and decided to send some one to
Yedo to see what could be done.   Kanzaki was
chosen and started off at once.   Though the officials
in Yedo had seen the ghosts so often, they were
much frightened to hear they had gone to Sakura,
fearing that if they did such horrible things there,
they would give still more trouble in Yedo.   Even my
lord Kozuke no Suke, bold though he was, was much
alarmed but as he had opposed the wishes of his ministers so long, he was far too obstinate to yield now so
he only smiled incredulously, and said : " The ghosts
used to come here quite often but they found they
could do no harm to me, and so they have gone to
Sakura to take leave of you before going back to their
home.   Let them alone.   They will trouble you no
more."   The officials were not a little encouraged by
their master's words and resolved to give up the idea
of establishing a temple.   In Sakura however, the
people were anxiously awaiting the return of the messenger feeling sure that he would bring a satisfactory
answer.   When therefore Kanzaki arrived and told
them what had taken place, they were greatly dis-
appointed, but Shinagawa who was present advanced,
and said : " As the spirits have been so often both
here and in Yedo, it is plain that some great misfortune
is threatening the house of our lord but he does not
comprehend his danger.   As they are spirits, we can

not say anything to them ; and so it seems to me that
the only way to appease them is for us to build a temple
for them.   Our lord is sure not to give his consent if
we ask him ; so the best way is for us to do it on our
own responsibility, without saying anything to him
about it ; and then, if he is angry afterwards when he
hears about it, I will bear all the blame."   All the
other officials gladly agreed to this and chose a place
where in old times the palace of Heishin no Masakado
had stood and roped it round at once.   The temple
was finished in a few days, a man named Hojuin made
head priest, and Sogoro was duly enshrined under the
name of " Sogo Daimyojin."   The ¡building of this
shrine perhaps soothed the spirits somewhat: for, after
it was finished, they never showed themselves again
in Sakura.

When the officials in Yedo heard that the shrine
had been built, they were all very glad and said:
" That is right, it is just what we wanted to do.   It
is not likely that the spirits will trouble us now."
My lord Kozuke no Suke however was not at all
pleased at it and summoned Hara, and said :   " You
have heard, haven't you, how the officials in Sakura
have built a temple and enshrined Sogoro there as
a god ?   Who started it ?   You asked me about it
some time since but I refused.   Surely you did not
send to Sakura after all and tell the people there to
build it.   It is very foolish of them to say that the
spirits have stopped their wanderings because Sogoro
has been made a god.   My high station made it impossible for them to revenge themselves on me, so

they took themselves off to Sakura and will not come
out any more now. It is absurd to make a temple and
enshrine them there after they had been driven away
by my good sword. What is the good of preparing
swords and spears when the war is all over?" Not
a little amazed and annoyed at being spoken to in
such a way, Hara said: "I admire your reason-
ing, but when you would not allow me to build the
temple, I of course had no way but to give up the idea.
I think the officials in Sakura must have planned it
themselves for I certainly did not authorize them to
do it." "Well then," said Kozuke no Suke, "go and
destroy it and if you find ·that any of the officials
have had a hand in it, you must punish them severely
for such audacious conduct."

That same night, after Hara had gone, the spirits of
Sogoro and his wife again appeared to my lord Kozuke
no Suke. He struck at them with his sword and they
vanished at once, but after that they appeared every
evening, till at last he was quite worn out, and his
health began to fail, and his days and months were
darkened with vain regrets.

Now Hara had gone to Sakura by his master's order
to ascertain who had had the temple built there in
Sogoro's honour. Immediately on his arrival, Shinagawa advanced and said: "It was all my own doing.
I did not consult with the other officials about it at
all. I have not been allowed to enter the presence
of our lord since I displeased him several years since;
so I shall be very glad if he summons me now and
thus permits me to see him once again. I am ready

to lay down my life for him whenever he requires it." Greatly pleased to hear he was so loyal, Hara went back and told his master all about it. My lord Kozuke no Suke was perhaps somewhat afraid of the spirits as they had appeared to him the very night he had sent Hara to Sakura; but any way he did not enquire any further about the temple.

CHAPTER XX.

Kozuke no Suke Kills Iwami no Kami and is Deprived of his Castle and Lands.

The Shogun's birthday was on the 11th. of the 10th. month (November 6th. 1649), and on that day an entertainment was given in the palace. To this my lord Kozuke no Suke was invited, and it chanced that as he was going along one of the corridors he met Iwami no Kami, who on seeing him at once bowed low and was stepping aside to let him pass when Kozuke no Suke called out in an angry tone: "You are an audacious fellow to follow me even here in the palace! I must show you what I can do!" So saying, he laid his hand on his sword. Iwami no Kami thinking it very strange, said: "Are you crazy?" Hardly had he spoken however when he

was cut down and fell to the ground. As it was night
and no one was prepared for such an occurrence nobody interfered for a few minutes, but soon there was
a great commotion and the cry was heard through all
the rooms : "Kozuke no Suke is fighting with Iwami
no Kami." This brought Kozuke no Suke to his
senses and he saw that he had killed Iwami no Kami
and felt great remorse for this his third victim.'
Thinking it dangerous to stay where he was, he ran
out. Every one in the palace was busy attending to
Iwami no Kami, and so no one followed him, and he
had no difficulty in making his way to the stable.
Finding his horse there, he jumped on its back and
galloped off as hard as he could go.

He rode the 12½ ri (about 80 miles) to Sakura in less
than three hours and roused the porter at the Gate, who
asked who was there. He replied : "I am Kozuke
no Suke, the lord of this castle. Be quick and open
the gate." Thinking it very strange that he should
come so far all alone, the porter instead of letting him
in, called the night watchman. He came at once and
seeing that it really was his master ordered them to
open the gate and going out to meet him, said : "I
am surprised to see you here all alone so late. If
you will wait a little, I will go and call the guard as
no doubt you wish to enter the castle by the main
entrance." Kozuke no Suke replied : "I have come
all the way here alone. Why should I want a guard
now ? Come with me." The porter took hold of the
horse's bridle and thus they entered the castle. The
retainers were all greatly astonished to see them and

collected in the large middle room. Kozuke no Suke summoned Shinagawa and consulted with him and Kanzaki in his private room. Truly sandal wood cannot be considered the same as other woods even if it is decayed. In the same way such a loyal man as Shinagawa could not but be consulted in preference to others in such an emergency, even though he had been under his lord's displeasure so long.

His lordship Iwami no Kami only lived a few hours after the fight in the palace; in fact, he died the next day, the 12th. at the early age of thirty-three. Many had heard him call out when he was attacked: "Are you mad Mr. Kozuke no Suke?" and it was clear to them that he had not quarreled, but unfortunately he was too severely wounded to speak, and had therefore in the eyes of the law been quarreling, and so all his dominions were confiscated; but the Shogun Iemitsu left directions on his deathbed that a dominion, yielding 20,000 koku at Matsuyama should be given to his oldest son.

As soon as it was known that his lordship Iwami no Kami was dead, a conference was held at the palace as to why Kozuke no Suke had gone to Sakura. Some said that he meant to rebel and advised that an army should be sent against him. While all the officials were consulting together as to who should lead the army, my lords Settsu no Kami and Yamato no Kami advanced, and said: "If you will leave it all to us, we will arrest him directly and bring him here without delay." As all the others approved, they obtained the necessary authority from the Shogun, and going to Sakura on the 13th, saw Kozuke no Suke. Settsu no Kami said to him : "Iwami no Kami who was wounded by you at the palace died yesterday morning. It was very wrong of you to flee here after having done such a thing, and it was almost decided to send an army against you; but as we are your relatives, we asked to be allowed to come and arrest you." Kozuke no Suke replied : "I am much obliged for your kindness, and am very sorry to have given you so much trouble ; but for the last five years, I have had a peculiar disease so that in the evening, I sometimes lose my senses and then people look like devils to me. During the first attack, I killed a maid and wounded a courtier who was a great favourite of mine and whose death I have regretted ever since. The next year I had another attack but I warned everybody to keep clear of me and so that year no harm was done. Since then I have been affected every winter, and recently I had another attack, brought on I think by the cold weather we have been having. His Lordship Iwami no Kami looked to me just like a devil, and so I lost my self-control and wounded him. I know that I am greatly to blame and do not expect to escape punishment, so please do not hesitate to do as you think best." Being his relatives, they knew all about his attacks and so did not need to question him further, but sent a messenger to Yedo, and then began to talk about other matters just as usual.

The officials in Yedo had just decided to send some others of their number to Sakura to arrest Kozuke no Suke when a messenger arrived from there with the

following note : " His Lordship Kozuke no Suke has
gone mad so we have put off examining him till he
recovers. We have arrested him and shall keep him
in custody till we hear from you what to do with him."
When the Shogun heard this, he ordered them to
bring him to Yedo at once; and so Kozuke no Suke
was taken there, and placed in the care of my lord
Tajima no Kami. His household was broken up and
his retainers dismissed, and my lord Settsu no Kami
was ordered to take charge of the castle of Sakura.
Thus a noble military house was destroyed by the
enmity of Sogoro and his wife, who had been so
cruelly oppressed by it. They had moreover caused
the death of my lord Iwami no Kami.

Some years later, His Lordship Hotta Sagami no
Kami, who belonged to another branch of the Hotta
family, moved to Sakura from Yamagata ; and at the
request of some of his descendants, the Emperor about
the year 1760, gave the name " Sogo Daimyojin " to
the temple that had been built on Mount Masakado in
honour of Sogoro and deified his four children under the
name of Yotsu no Miya Gongen ; and that temple has
guarded Sakura ever since. Twice every year, in the
spring and in the autumn, festivals are held there and
are always well attended ; and whenever the lord of the
District returns from a journey, he always visits the
temple before going to his castle. How true it is that
man's worship increases the power of the gods, and the
gods' favour increases the happiness of man. Ever
since this time the town of Sakura has flourished ; and
we are glad to say that evil has decreased and good

TEMPLE NEAR SAKURA IN HONOUR OF SOGORO.

Page 189.

fortune has smiled on all the families and households
in the District; and so we believe that Sogoro deserves
to be honoured as much now as in the past.

www.ingramcontent.com/pod-product-compliance
Lightning Source LLC
Chambersburg PA
CBHW030828020726
47499CB00006B/2113